James Warlow

Faith, Its Pleasures, Trials, and Victories

And other Poems

James Warlow

Faith, Its Pleasures, Trials, and Victories
And other Poems

ISBN/EAN: 9783337207076

Printed in Europe, USA, Canada, Australia, Japan

Cover: Foto ©Andreas Hilbeck / pixelio.de

More available books at **www.hansebooks.com**

FAITH

ITS PLEASURES TRIALS AND VICTORIES

And Other Poems

BY

JAMES WARLOW

LONDON
LONGMANS, GREEN, AND CO
1882

Ballantyne Press
BALLANTYNE, HANSON AND CO.
EDINBURGH AND LONDON

CONTENTS.

———o———

To the Reader.

FAITH, here, is like a mountain range, whose
    peaks alone are seen,
But glorious are the valleys that lie those peaks
    between ;
The heights explored, survey the plains, and rest
    your weary feet,—
Each covert gleams with beauty and with flowers
    most rare and sweet.
Perchance, a little while elapsed, we'll 'midst their
    fragrance rove,
And wander further on the way hedged in by Peace
    and Love.

FAITH.

—o—

Part First.

THE Poem opens with an invocation to Faith for illumination and strength. Allusion to a deceased parent ; his Faith and constancy. The sceptic who sneers at Faith possesses it, as also does everything living in some degree. Allusion to scientific men who pretend to extraordinary knowledge. The ability to prove the simplest thing questioned. Human knowledge limited, though its limits may not be reached. Reason and Faith are not enemies, but labour together and mutually assist each other. Faith's power unites the past and present and shows as living those who, humanly speaking, are dead. Earnestness necessary to gain Faith. The Faith of triflers and mere professors not to be relied on. The real Christian's armour wanting by such at Death, though they may then conquer by believing. Early instruction in Truth likely to assist Faith. Sad effects of such instruction being despised. Faith can save and reason. God, the great First Cause, cannot be found out. God finds man and gives him His Word for his guidance. Man is taught by the Spirit if taught aright. Unbelief born of ignorance. Man cannot know all in the flesh, but with meekness and Faith must wait upon God. Faith brings not evil but good to man. Faith whilst leading to future bliss sheds temporal blessings. Benighted condition of countries where the true Faith is not known. Allusion to a recent visit to Uganda. Britain formerly in a similar state to Uganda. Whence Britain's present power. Scientific men should acknowledge the power of God, who beareth rule and whose glorious Kingdom is nigh.

Part First.

PARENT of Hope, offspring of Love Divine,
  May thy pure torch with holy radiance shine —
Illume and strengthen, for my heart would raise
A simple song to celebrate thy ways.
If but one wavering soul my Muse may find—
One struggling pilgrim, with o'erburdened mind—
One hapless wretch, to Love and Hope a foe—
One doubting heart, made doubtful by its woe—
And bring it safe beneath thy glorious wing,
Happy I'll be, nor will I cease to sing.

      *   *   *   *   *

O thou, my Father! numbered with the blest.
Thy certain Faith hath found eternal rest ;
'Twas thou, that first, my infant spirit led
To trust in Him, who for His creatures bled.
'Twas from thy lips, the earnest prayer arose,
Ere dewy eve did our young eyelids close : —
Methinks again I hear thy solemn tone
Steal through the air, as here I sit alone ;

I see thy upturned face, so calm, so pale,
Beseeching Him, whose promises ne'er fail.
No flowery path thro' this cold world hadst thou,
Yet cheerful Hope sat ever on thy brow ;
And when o'er others came a saddening gloom,
And when they saw great clouds of sorrow loom
In dim futurity—thou didst with them pray,
And bid them hope for brighter, happier day.
Strong as the sun, thy steadfast Faith sublime,
Burst thro' the gloom and cheered pale sorrow's time,
Nor ever left thee, in the darkest hour,
The sport of worldlings, or of Fortune's power.
And when that eve arrived, that solemn eve,
When thou wast called thy worldly home to leave,
When chill thy frame and icy-cold thy brow,
Wiped by the hand that pens these numbers now,
No terrors came thy waking soul to fright,
But thy bright Faith breathed calmly a " Good-night."
Thy heav'n-bound spirit had its prison fled
Long ere I knew I only clasped the dead.

*   *   *   *   *

Immortal Faith—Death is but Life to thee,
Stripes are like kisses—sorrows, joys to be,

Upheld by thee, no power the soul can move,
Blest with assurance of Eternal Love.

*   *   *   *   *

But what *is* Faith ? the withering sceptic sneers,—
With outward boldness cloaking inward fears—
In ignorance lost, or if, more vicious still,
Should selfish pleasures work in him their will,
Bearing his spirit down—or if his mind,
Careless of Truth, false theories should blind ;
Has he *no* Faith ? though he attempts a sneer
Whene'er the word is whispered in his ear !
Come, Sceptic ! come !   Thy tinsel cast aside,
Search for pure Gold,—the universe is wide,—
Think not thy mind so meanly clad or bare,
Truth's priceless garments doth at present wear,
Thy Life's a lie ! if be, thy tongue speaks true,
Thy every action proves Faith dwells in you.
Yes ! he has Faith ! and so the Sparrow hath,
Whose willing wings beat on their airy path,
While she conveys the bit of moss or hay,
To form her nest upon *some future* day.
The Ants have Faith, and build their curious home,
Lay in their store for many weeks to come ;
The Bee, instinctive, marks the coming frost,
And, ceaseless, labours ere the Summer's lost.

The very beasts, with natures unsubdued,
Put by a morsel for their young ones' food.
Yea, all that live, or insect, beast, or bird,
Possess *some* Faith, by which their Life is stirred.
They think they'll live, or why the present pains?
Their acts prove Faith, and hence their future gains.

But these have *instinct* only, nor can deal
With aught but what their senses see or feel;
No Reason guides them in the lowly sphere,
No calm Reflection curbs their strange career,
Or these possessing, still, they but extend
To few days only—then must have an end.

But man! with Nature's crown upon thy brow,
Hast thou no Faith? of all creation thou?
Bold in thy thoughts, with speculation rife,
Thou e'en wouldst prove the hidden spring of Life,
Fain wouldst thou demonstrate, by thine own might,
How particles with particles unite!
Wouldst probe thyself, in vain attempt to find
How matter's wove so curiously with mind!
These failing,—thy vexation, or thy pride,
Thou dost in scientific verbiage hide,
Or, may be, dost with bold assertion say—
" Poor wretches we—mere animated clay."

Vain man of Science, wise in ignorance,
Thy studies tend but to confuse—perchance
Thy search for knowledge is sincere, if so,
Seek, first, the sources whence *thy* powers flow,
And if those sources are beyond thy ken,
In fairness, own thy ignorance to men ;
For causes are not, where effects are seen
And life lies hid, where thy thoughts ne'er have been !

*   *   *   *   *

See yon broad lands, which verdant grass o'er-
     spreads,
There the sweet spring-flowers hide their modest
     heads,—
The spring-flowers, known to ev'ry girl and boy,
And gathered oft, in simple, childish joy.
Come, pluck a blade of grass, and there, behold !
Close by is, glitt'ring, many a cup—like gold !
Well, gather some—then use thy knowledge great,
What seems an easy thing to demonstrate.
That blade of grass is *green*, and yet close by
A *yellow* buttercup peeps at the sky.
Come now, Professor,—if I'm not too bold—
Why is one green ?   Why is the other gold ?

The same sweet dew falls both on grass and flower,
The same sun shines on each, — each feels the
    power
Of wind and rain, each has its humble birth,
And each is nourished by the self-same earth.
Now take the flower home, and take the grass,
Dissect with care—nor one corpuscle pass
Unnoticed by ; their juices magnify
And test, and all their hidden germs descry ;
Study with care, a week—a month—a year,
Then answer, for a simple bard would hear
Thy speech, if be, in all that time thou'st seen—
Thy mind assenting—why the grass is green ?
Produce their living essence, if you can,
Then try to solve that greater mystery—man ?
Alas ! methinks your learnèd brain can give
But mere opinions how these frail things live ;
That springing blade—that tender flower contains
Secrets as dark as earth's remotest veins.
And mind's great waves, like ocean's, have their
    bounds,
Nor ere will here burst o'er forbidden grounds ;
There is, where human knowledge ne'er can rise,
Where Understanding fails—Perception dies.

This may not yet be reached—The ambient field
Of Truth may yet a further harvest yield;
A seeming accident or thought may turn
A page in Nature's book, where we may learn
Numberless facts which ne'er our minds conceived,
Philosophy advanced or, possible, believed.

*   *   *   *   *

'Tis at this point, when Reason's power declines,
Faith's pinions rise—her lamp more brightly shines;
Brother and Sister, hand-in-hand they've roved,
Intricate paths by each alike beloved.
Faith aiding Reason thro' the glimm'ring night,
Reason supporting Faith when dawns the light:
Ne'er did true Faith—true Reason's voice despise,
Ne'er did true Reason fail with Faith to rise.

*   *   *   *   *

Thy glorious power, majestic Faith, unites
Eternity with eternity, lights
The dead past, with glittering gems of love,
Memorials of Peace, from Heaven above.
Leads the lone soul—for lone the soul must be—
Though friends around us ev'ry hour we see—
To blissful seats already filled by those
Whose loving hearts, for us, in prayer oft rose.

Anon ! we breathe a Parent's cherished name,
We feel his love an ever-present flame,
Our *living* Parent, though for long years dead,
And pillowed 'neath the sod his lowly head.
We see our children whom we've laid to rest,
And press them fondly to our heaving breast.

Still further back, through age, and age, we speed,—
On living Promises, in joy, we feed ;
Faith leads the way—and back the ages roll,
Whilst God speaks peace unto the earnest soul.

For 'tis the *earnest* soul alone can hope
To gain sweet Faith, or with dark doubt to cope.
No thoughtless trifler ere her treasures found,
Or basked in peace upon her sacred ground.
Deep in the mind, the Understanding lies,
From depths of thought pure Faith must take her
        rise ;
The vicious, slothful, and the ignorant—
The hearers and the talkers of mere cant—
Professed Believers, whose glib tongue can preach
What ne'er they knew—who can with safety teach
Accected doctrines, chapters read, sing hymns,
And lull to sleep the soul imbued with sins ;

These may have Faith—but will their faith survive,
When Death's dread moments to their souls arrive?

Momentous question! let us pause awhile,
In that lone hour can mere Professors smile?
When stripped of all the garish things of life,
They, shiv'ring, linger from the certain strife.
Will false Philosophy assist them now?
Or past professions smooth their haggard brow?
Down from their shoulders falls the loathsome
    dress,
And flesh! and spirit! quiver in distress!
Truth's snowy girdle 'circles not his soul
Whose breastplate's pierced with many rents and
    foul!
Where is that shield impregnable, whose sight
Scares the dark enemy of Love and Light?
Has he that Helmet, glorious to behold,
To be desired before broad fields of gold?
Alas! no helmet his damp forehead shields,
Nor joy, nor hope, his palsied brain now yields.
Where is that sword, well-tempered, from the skies?
Alas! in dust the glittering weapon lies;
His skill-less arm no thrust at Death can give,
Nor teach the monster how a man may live.

Yet in that hour Despair need not presume
A certain conquest, or a settled doom;
A beaming eye which pitying Love o'erflows,
Sees the keen pangs and waits to grant repose;
And living words in anxious accents cry,
"Turn thee! Believe! O wherefore wouldst thou
     die!"

Believe! Perchance an Echo sad and faint,
Across the heart one streak of Hope may paint;
One feeble ray from childhood's precious days,
A Father's warning, or a Mother's praise,
As they, when in his innocence and youth,
With Love admired and taught the way of Truth;
Long ere his pride and worldly-wisdom led
His mind—his soul—to things decayed and dead.

But stay! again I pause; methinks I hear
A cry of mingled agony and fear;
A cloud of Phantoms gather round his Sprite,
Blot the lone ray, and all again is night!
His Father's warning long had been despised,
His Mother's teaching never had been prized;
They'd read but little—simple folk of trade,
Reading and study he'd a hobby made;

They knew enough his boyhood's growth to
    scan—
Had helped to rear him to the age of man—
Their stock of knowledge then he overhauled,
And far beyond in darksome labyrinths crawled ;
And learned enough to doubt, alas ! no more ;
The " still small voice " was lost in worldly lore.

So now, instead of Parents, Phantoms rise,
A horrid host, and blind his mental eyes ;
Here Hume in subtle argument appears,
And selfish Hobbs leads asses by the ears ;
Here mad Vanina mourns his cruel fate—
Payne and Voltaire their rhapsodies relate ;
And monkey-men from France and other lands,
Dance, jabbering on, their souls within their hands.
Lucretius—Poet, seer,—amongst the rest,
Hopes with the beasts, to be for ever blest,
Attunes with impious hand the sacred lyre,
To themes which only demons could inspire.
Anon ! a crowd of mock believers howl,—
And drunken Parsons nodding o'er the bowl—
And loathsome hypocrites with faces long
To suit themselves drawl forth a pious song.

Such authors he had read—such men had seen—
Still deadly host they stand him and his Faith between

Come forth, sweet Spirit, from thy heavenly home,
Seraphic Faith, into his spirit come!
Shine thro' the gloom, which doth so darkly lower,
The future's his—if only for an hour.
Thou ne'er didst hang upon a broken stem;
Display thyself, thy power will scatter them.
Thou too can'st reason, reason with him now,
And Life, not Death, shall hover o'er his brow.

*   *   *   *   *

That God must be on every heart is sealed,
That Christ is God, by God hath been revealed;
And this one God, to thoughtful minds must mean,
The great First Cause on which all else doth lean:
By whom are all things—in whose glorious hand
Systems and suns are grasped as grains of sand.
Intelligence Eternal, pervading
In some degree all life or living thing!
Incomprehensible and infinite—
Filling all space, all matter, darkness, light;
A Spirit—moving each and every way,
Yet boundless! endless! all the vast display

Of suns, or stars, or earth, or man, or mind,
A mere atom of the Deity! find
Out our God, who can?

                    Can any seed
Of grain, or flow'ring plant, or noisome weed,
When it springs up, find out the power or hand
That left it erst beneath the sheltering land?
You answer, no! Ah! how much less can we
By searching, find Eternal Majesty?

Yet God finds us, and gives to us His Word,
And spirit-taught, our inmost souls are stirred;
If we despise His Word, how can we know,
The glorious Presence, the seraphic glow?
If man by man be guided, man may fall—
If God shall guide, then man surmounts the pall,
And leaves his body and his dust behind,
Gives God his all—his spirit, soul and mind;
For what is body, but a nice machine,
Moved by a spirit,—all unknown, unseen?
Unknown unto ourselves—though some conceive,
That they know all—the unknown disbelieve;
For unbelief of Ignorance is born,
Nourished by Pride, that flesh-engendered thorn.

                                       c

To disbelieve what we don't comprehend
Is to deny our birth, our life, our end ;
And he who will know all, that can be known
Of any given thing—or life, or stone,
Must know the nature of all things that be
In heaven, in earth, in air, in space, in sea !
And as such knowledge ne'er can be possessed
By soul confined in a material breast,
That soul must wait upon the great First Cause,
With childlike Faith, to understand His laws ;
History, and daily experience, shows,
From meekest minds the truest knowledge flows ;
Vain Pride, or self-conceit, need ne'er expect
To be with Truth's fair garment ere bedecked.

Can that thing see, which ne'er possessed an eye ?
Can that thing move, which passive ere must lie ?
Can that perceive, which nothing knows of mind ?
Can that thing lead—which in itself is blind ?
No ! nor can man or think, or move aright,
Without Faith's eye to penetrate the night ;
Faith leads our minds from error's winding ways,
And crowns with joyful Hope, dim Future's days.

*   *   *   *   *

What do'st thou ask, O Faith! that men should strive
To rob thee of thy sweet prerogative?
Dost thou desire the human race to die—
Dost thou support oppressive tyranny—
Dost thou uphold foul cruelty or war,—
Teach Death to ride on iron bolts afar—
Encourage Vice to blot fair Virtue's name,
To smother in the breast her holy flame—
To live to self a mean, soul-killing life,
When want and wo amidst our friends are rife?
Dost thou delight in weak or rotten states—
Time-serving Rulers—partial magistrates—
In justice cloaked—the itching palm to gild—
In wolfish rogues, with outsides fair and mild?
Dost thou delight vile alcohol to see
Make mankind beasts—fill homes with misery—
Dost with thee bring a pestilence or blight—
Drag fire and sword from out the realms of night?
Dost thou claim superstition for thine own—
Or dost thou cause the sacrificial groan
Torn from the suffering heathen's livid lips,
When frenzied Priest's dread knife his life-blood
    sips?
Ah no! far from such things thou dost remove;
They're born of Hell—thou'rt born of Light and Love.

'Tis theirs to lash for sin with varying pain,
'Tis thine to heal the bleeding stripes again.
'Tis theirs to teach what evil is and wrath,
Thine to illume sweet mercy's flowery path;
Their presence proves man is from God astray,
Thy finger points the new and living way
Whereby he may recover all his loss,
Find peace with God—and glory in the Cross.

Avaunt! ye teachers who would steal away
Our glorious Faith—our life-sustaining ray!
Bright Truth's proud enemies and mankind's foes,
In Tyndall's " moods and tenses," seek repose;
And when your spirit's troubled billows rise—
When waves of thought half blind your inward eyes,
Turn to the senseless earth and grasp a clod,
Ask it for Peace, and mock the living God!
But teach not thoughtless men to do the same,
Though twenty letters supplement your name.

     *   *   *   *   *

Thy power benign, O holy Faith, surrounds
This life's rough turmoil with angelic sounds;
Whilst leading on to glorious bliss to come,
Prosperous the land wherein thou find'st a home;

It's simple peasants live in royal state,

Compared with heathen kings on whom poor
heathens wait.

Turn we to Afric's sunny land to see

How mankind thrives where nothing's known of thee ;

Or what is known is just enough to raise,

The gloomy mind a log or tree to praise.

To Mtessi grand—Uganda's mighty king,

Important news the bloody hangmen bring,—

For such his messengers.—"There comes," they say,

"A stranger, pale, from country far away;

He comes with gifts—nor doth he come alone,

To see our King, and bow before his throne."

Great Mtessi smiles in triumph—see him stand

With rolling eyeballs 'midst his sable band :

His stalwart frame, half naked, who can scan,

And doubt, but Mtessi is a king of man.

He deigns to look—great Mtessi looks around—

All other eyes are bent upon the ground,—

Seven sun-baked walls surround his palace great,

His wretched hut of dignity and state ;

A hundred wives on mighty Mtessi call,

Great Mtessi's proud—for he can feed them all ;

A glorious scene his brilliant orbs contain—
A thousand huts lie scattered o'er the plain;
And thrice that number of dependent braves
Wait his command to plough the stormy waves
Of inland lakes—or seize the bow and spear
Should Mtessi's foes attempt to venture near.
His Fleet majestic close at anchor rides,
Two score canoes, with stained or painted sides,
Of bark well fashioned and by skilful hands,
Fitted with paddles for his warlike bands.
" Let them approach," he said, " Great Mtessi's power,
Was ere supreme as at the present hour !
Uganda's king the stranger's eye may see—
And blood of men shed to his honour be."

The stranger meets the king—a Briton bold,
He comes to view the secret land of gold ;
Uganda's lakes and plains and mountains wild,
A glorious home for nature's darkest child ;
In minerals rich, and rich in precious stones,
And rich, alas ! in death and bleaching bones.
Wealth in each rock—each broken lump they meet,
Gleaming with ore, is spurned by negro feet.
Here is material, and strength, and youth,
But power is wanting, for they lack the Truth ;

And thus Uganda will thy riches lie,
Till tempests bare them to thy blazing sky,
Or till thy horrid superstitions cease,
In Knowledge, Faith, and holy Gospel Peace,
For temporal blessings fall from Wisdom's wings,
Wisdom from Truth, which from the Eternal springs.

As stealthy Lion, with suspicious glare,
Moves slowly backward to his hidden lair—
From right to left his fiery glances dart—
Whilst, fearful, the tangly creepers seem to start—
So, watchful, stepped Uganda's dusky king,
Back to his throne ; around, a savage ring
Of courtiers stand expectant ; in the shade
By yon plantation of Bananas made,
Waiting their doom, a groaning group surveys
The royal pageants—the superb displays—
" Look ! " cried the king—aloft the cry is borne,
And thirty cords from thirty turbans torn,
And thirty strangling wretches' dying shrieks
Blanch the pale bronze upon the Briton's cheeks.

And thus Uganda's monarch proves his power,
By strangling thirty men in half an hour.

    *   *   *   *   *

Time was when all the world in ignorance lay,

Dark as Uganda's at the present day ;

E'en Britain's soil, now from such horrors free,

Drank streams of gore shed just as wantonly ;

Priests in her Groves their helpless victims tied,

Stuck deep their knives, and watched them till they
          died ;

Marked how the blood from their gashed bowels flowed,

With lies pretending that the Future showed

By its red streak what stores of bad or good,

She held for those who round the victim stood.

Vain nonsense ! yet though now no blood be shed,

What myriads cling to superstitions dead.

Whence came thy power, Great Britain ? whence thy
          might ?

From Heaven's high King,—borne on the Gospel's
          light ;

Thy honoured sons, whose genius sheds round thee,

A halo bright of immortality,

Ne'er of themselves, His hidden laws could scan,

But, taught of Him, they taught their fellow-man ;

With trembling saw His footstep's glorious tread,

Showed it to us, then slumbered 'midst the dead.

*   *   *   *   *

'Tis those alone whose spirits ask He feeds,
From Wisdom's store to tell mankind its needs ;
And when their minds, reflecting on His laws,
Trace what *is* seen, to unseen distant cause ;
'Tis God in answer to a longing sprite
Instils a ray of pure superior light ;
The nations then the noble gift applaud,
The servant honour, and—forget the Lord.

   * * * * *

Arise, ye men of Science ! own His power !
Your Life's a span, a troubled fleeting hour ;
You pin to others' thoughts your own, and must,
Full half your learning's taken upon trust ;
Too short your days the simplest thing to prove,
Save this—that God exists with Truth and Love.

   * * * * *

He beareth rule ! whose glorious Kingdom's nigh,
Whose Son commands the legions of the sky ;
Whose Holy Spirit points the way to Life,
Whilst Faith, triumphant, scatters sin and strife !
He beareth Rule ! His Saints will find a home,
Come ! Israel's Hope ! Thy children's prayer is
   " Come ! "

             D

Part Second.

MANY things we know of are sweet, but the joy brought by Faith surpasses all. Address to money-seekers, who, while bedecking themselves and their houses, neglect the nobler part of their nature. Such use their souls as a tyrant would a captive. Their own consciences will heap curses. Address to Faith. The world is envious and attempts to destroy what Heaven sends for the good of men. Faith was, and still is, attacked by the world. The joy and beauty of those who sleep in Faith cannot be known here, though sometimes a glimpse of Heaven is vouchsafed. Stephen's testimony and glorious martyrdom. Allusions to Nero, to the burning of Rome, and to some of those martyred in Nero's reign. Faith gives Fortitude. Could we see what angels behold, our minds and affections would be changed. Allusions to the martyrdom of Ignatius, Justin, Polycarp, Felicitates and her sons ; allusion to Sextus and Laurentius. Sextus' prophecy. Laurentius' boldness ; his terrible though glorious death. Allusion to the martyrdom of 300 Christians, to the Theban Legion who refuse to adore idols. The Emperor Maximian's rage. He decimates the Legion. The soldiers' death and Faith's victory. Faith's dangers do not lie in Persecution, but in ease and luxury. Priestly murderers, their trial near at hand. Allusion to Ridley, to Latimer, to Hawkes, and to Cranmer. A time of Persecution is preferable to a time when Faith is inactive. It matters little what the different Churches or Sects pretend. The Scriptures free. To understand the Truth seekers should forget the Schools and study God's Word with prayer. The Spirit's teaching to be preferred. Forms and Ordinances only shadows. God our only trust ; His Word our only Guide. Mankind of every age entreated to accept the blessings of Faith ere it be too late. Allusion to Jacob and Edom, and the near approach of the end.

Part Second.

SWEET is the Cuckoo's voice in early spring,
　　Sweet are the flowers to which the dew-drops
　　　cling.
Sweet is the breeze to convalescent's cheek,
Sweet 'tis to aid the troubled, lone and weak.
Sweet is the dawn of Love in maiden's breast ;
And sweet the kisses by a mother pressed—
But sweeter far than these the joy that's given,
When Faith directs the weary soul to heaven.

＊　　＊　　＊　　＊　　＊

Scrape on, ye sons of mammon—burrow deep,
Bedeck your earth-holes—gather, eat and sleep ;
What profit have you when the sere leaf sheds
Its withered form upon your earth-bound heads ?
The grave cannot preserve you, slow decay
Consumes with worms—consumed you pass away.
O fools and blind ! the dainty flesh you prize,
Is mere corruption when your spirit flies !

Then why, if Reason sits upon her throne,
Should men, by acts, these mighty truths disown ;

Why feed and clothe the meaner part, and keep
The nobler naked, starving?   Could you sleep
In peace and know a dark and dreadful night
Was evermore to last—nor sun, nor light
Of any kind was ever more to gleam—
Or your keen eye discover one faint beam
On things surrounding?   Would you grope and feel
For showy dress, or find your highest weal
In grasping gold and fing'ring jewels rare
While everlasting night broods everywhere?
Yet without Faith your soul's vast future's dark,
All unenlivened by the faintest spark,
While all your days this world's vain dross employs,
Neglecting that which leads to endless joys.

How would that man, that tyrant's power detest,
Who'd dragged him from his home, his bride, his
        rest,—
Enclosed him in a cell, with outside grand,
But inside lined with slush and dirt and sand;
Who drowns his captive's pleadings and his moans
In laughter wild or giddy music's tones?—
Yet thus, O worldly careless ones, ye use
Your precious souls, and your own-selves abuse.

Think not to say, you have no inward pain,
That you rejoice in Pleasure, Lust, and Gain ;
Lie not to your own consciences—'tis they
Ere long with pangs will sweep your lies away :
Heap on your heads an everlasting curse,
And show you, naked, to the Universe.

O Faith sublime ! that consummation dread
Reserve for few ; thine influences shed
Abroad, so that the careless throng may see,
Their present pleasures tend to misery.
Let Wisdom's lamp this chequered life illume,
While thine, lights this and that beyond the tomb ;
Wisdom her children consecrates by thee,
To life and joy through all eternity ;
And, here, the sweetest blessings shed around
And proves the beauties of thy hallowed ground.
And though, at times, the road be rough and steep,
Although, at times, the timid ones may weep,
Rougher the road, more glorious the prize ;
Tears shed for thee, fall diamonds from the eyes.

    *   *   *   *   *

When aught from Heaven, this fallen world perceives,
With envious wrath her inmost bosom heaves ;

She watches well its path, with envious glare
Vends poisoned sweets, and lays her cunning snare;
Now tempting gifts she offers—now with frowns
Shows reeking knife, and martyrs' fiery crowns;
And uses all her skill to drag to earth
That which she sees to be of nobler birth;
And oft the heavenly visitant appears,
Charmed with her kisses or subdued with fears.

'Twas thus with thee, O Faith! when hither sent,
The world's strong-bow 'gainst thy fair form was bent—
And those whose hearts thy holy Love embraced,
With fire and sword, through land and sea were
　　　　　chased—
Consigned to dungeons, or on gibbets high
Gave up the ghost, in blissful agony.
And thus 'tis still, though now in subtler forms,
A wicked world thy shining stronghold storms.

　　　　*　　　*　　　*　　　*　　　*

O what peculiar brilliancy will glow
Round those who nourished thee in pain below!
What joys they feel, who erst have been oppress'd,
But who now lean on the Eternal's breast,
'Tis not for us to know, nor can we think
Till we with them life's blessèd waters drink,

Though sometimes ere Death's dreaded shade draws
    nigh
A glimpse of Heaven may cheer a favoured eye.

The first ripe grape in Faith's fair cluster found,
Since men and angels hailed the Gospel's sound,
In Stephen see, whose sin-accusing breath
Caused teeth to gnash and crowds desire his death.
Lo! whilst his earnest spirit bids them know,
God's Holy One was murdered here below,
Wide ope the heavens—in awful glory grand
That Holy One at God's right hand doth stand.
What Majesty with His can we compare,
Incomparable smiles His glances share,
Oceans of Love His beaming features heave
For those, who, left behind, He'll never leave.

    *   *   *   *   *

But since at Stephen's daring breast were thrown,
The rugged missile and relentless stone:
Since, in his flesh, the gaping wounds conveyed
His agony to those for whom he prayed—
O what a glorious army has aspired
To prove by Death how Faith their zeal hath fired;
Strong men and maidens, youth and tott'ring age,
Have writ in blood their Faith on golden page.

                                    E

Hark! from Macæna's tower, where Nero stands,
With tuneful harp within his blood-stained hands,
The song of burning Troy is sung aloud,
Whilst fire and death lap up the Roman crowd;
Whilst hissing flames through Rome's great circus
        leaps
And palaces destroyed lie shapeless heaps;
His servants' work done at their chief's command,
That coward leader of a Pagan Band.
Yet not content with what the fire consumed
Though thousands in its furnace were entombed,
This child of Hell in fear and anger swept
His cruel rage where Christians watched and wept.
O'er guiltless heads his reeking weapon drew,
In vain to hide his crimes, with crimes anew;
And Persecution's torch shone down the road
Where gleeful demons flocked from dark abode!

O woeful spectacle! the children cling
To mother's neck in fearful wondering:
Then from her clasping arms are ruthless torn
Dashed 'gainst the rocks, while she is left to mourn,
Until the faggots blaze before her eyes,
And she a heap of smouldering ashes lies.

See how these dogs are fighting which shall feast,
On what appears to be a savage beast—
Now the rough skin is rent, and now the gore
Streams through the hide and dyes the cursèd floor;
List! how terribly human sounds that moan,
Alas! a Christian in that skin is sewn.
Yet holy Faith e'en these dread trials stands—
With scorn surveys the power of heathen bands;
And when proud Nero thought her life was gone
She, stronger, rose and brighter victories won.

O Fortitude sublime, by sweet Faith given,
Thy glorious fruits adorn the highest heaven.
Well hast thou fought the everlasting fight
And reaped thy harvest in the fields of Light,
Death must succumb when Faith and thee combine,
But Truth must flourish, Holiness must shine.

* * * * *

Could we but see what angels now behold,
How would our faces shine, our speech grow bold!
No wavering thought our bosom would contain,
No doubtful musings work within our brain;
But holy confidence our souls pervade—
Forgetting self, we'd fly to others' aid,

The power to sin, in black oblivion hurled,
What new and constant Love would fill the world ;
As Truth arose, all flesh would welcome pain,
And every pang would bring immortal gain.

Such sight Ignatius had, whose infant charms,
Were blessed and fondled in the Saviour's arms ;
His zealous Faith, so holy, calm, and sure,
The greatest torments gladly did endure ;
His noble spirit gained the wished repose,
And, crowned with martyr's crown, in glory rose !
And such had Justin, Truth's great champion he,
Who stoutly fought 'gainst false Philosophy ;
Men's lies he proved,—Truth's priceless treasures
found,
Ere he fell, murdered, on the bloodstained ground ;
And venerable Polycarp in prayer,
Resigned this life, Heaven's beauteous home to share.

Felicitates of illustrious name,
And shining virtues to the Saviour came ;
Laid at His feet her own—her children's life,
Whilst heathen swords flashed gory from the strife.
Two of her sons before her eyes were bound,
And dreadful war-clubs dashed their brains around,

A third, who to his holy Faith still clung,
From giddy precipice was madly flung ;
Another scourged, then pressed by weights to death,
His mangled body cursed by Pagan breath.
And other three, with her, beheaded lie,
Their lustrous spirits mounting to the sky.
Eight living monuments her household gave,
Of Faith triumphant o'er the darkest grave.

*   *   *   *   *

What glorious hosts in those dark, early, days,
Sowed Faith in blood, and reaped their Maker's praise !
Bright, living, trophies of the power divine,
Immortal honours round their brows entwine !

See Sextus dying,—Rome's great Bishop he,—
Would now such men held that benighted See—
To good Laurentius pass the solemn word,
(Which he believed the moment that he heard),
" Three days, Laurentius, and on Heaven's bright plain,
I'll meet thee—never more to part again."
Prophetic message ! did the Saint's cheek pale
At thought of death, or did his courage fail ?
No failing courage looks or words betray,
A Christian's hope his actions all display.

And when the heathen Ruler bade him bring,
The Church's treasures for his Pagan King,
Nobly and fearlessly Laurentius brought
The poorest of his flock by Wisdom taught —
" Here are the treasures, Christ's Church owns below —
Say ! richer treasures can I ever show ! "
Dark lowered the heathen's brow with rage and scorn,
Whilst bold Laurentius from the place was torn ;
Unutterable tortures wracked his frame,
Yet Faith maintained her heart-sustaining flame ;
And when his broken limbs slow fire consumed,
Her beauteous bud, a lovely blossom bloomed,
And pure Laurentius' spirit passed away,
To share with Sextus heaven's eternal day.

    *   *   *   *   *

Where smokes that mighty kiln of burning lime,
Come ! see a sight ! to Angels' eyes sublime !
Three hundred Christians on its dread brink stand,
With thrice three thousand Pagans close at hand ;
" Adore our gods," —the raging heathens cry—
" To great Jove sacrifice, or else ye die."
With one accord the holy band unite,
Faith's power to prove, her undiminished might—
With one accord, within the burning mass,
Three hundred heroes their last trial pass.

Again, a wonder see! by Faith 'tis wrought—
'Midst savage hordes, her virtues still are taught,—
Through Gaul's broad fields the rage of battle
          tears,
And streaming blood her channels wider wears.
Maximian's hosts her fairest plains o'errun,
And Roman fires leap ruddier than the sun:
(War has to heathen minds uncommon charms,
The gods abide, they think, with those in arms).
But say! whilst all the mighty camp's ablaze!
Whilst barbarous hosts the shout exultant raise!
And rend the air with their loved idols' names,
And bind the sacrifice 'midst swords and flames!
Why in the shadow stand that legion stern,
And from the scene their rugged features turn
Silent and sad? whilst o'er their armour bright
Flit eddying waves of smoke and lurid light;
That sad, stern legion,—'tis the Theban band,
True to the Faith in conq'ring pagans' land.
Though great the victories their trusty swords
Have gained for Rome over opposing hordes,
Yet will they not 'midst Rome's resistless power,
Adore Rome's idols for a single hour;
Yet will they not against a Christian raise,
A sword or spear for either death or praise;

They cry—a legion o'er six thousand strong—
"Our steel for Rome—our souls to Christ belong."

This to Rome's Emperor—Maximian's rage—
A faithful picture of a faithless age—
Forgetful of their services, and scars
Received for him in many hard-fought wars,
Commands that one in ev'ry ten be slain
To test the Faith of those who then remain ;
A bloody test, though glorious in the end,
Each man remaining cheers his doomèd friend ;
In fury and surprise Maximian finds
How weak his power o'er Truth-enlightened minds.
Then through the ranks his cruel mandate ran,
And fell that glorious legion to a man ;
Proving by death, how vain the Roman's boasts,
How weak the strength of this world's mightiest
      hosts—
Nor heathen rage—nor Satan's jealous might
The hardy blossom of Faith's tree could blight.

    *   *   *   *   *

Yes ! Fierce the storms that hailed thy Gentile birth,
And rude the cradle formed for thee on earth ;
No feathery down made soft thy infant bed,
O'er thorns and briars thy tender feet were led ;

In heavy chains thy meek-eyed youth abode,
And Fancy saw thee bending 'neath the load ;
And oft, perchance, a solitary fear,
Might warn thy soul that man's great foe was near,
Till in his face thy rattling chains were flung,
And majesty severe around thee hung.
Thy dangers ne'er in persecutions lay,
They haunt soft Luxury's road and smoothest way.

Yes ! Ease and Luxury ! ye subtle foes !
How deadly yet how cherished your repose ;
More deadly to the soul than aught beside,
A pregnant curse, a road both smooth and wide ;
Ye lull the flesh-bound soul to sleep of death,
And hell's narcotic fumes taint every breath.
Peace ! peace ! ye sing, in ever-pleasing tones,
Whilst Peace replies—"Ah no !" with sighs and
    groans.
There is no peace, when Faith is lulled to sleep,
And Wisdom ling'ring waits and Truth doth weep.

     *   *   *   *   *

Ye priestly murderers—bedecked and fine,
Whose tongues are mellow as your ruby wine,
How bravely ye, your shelt'ring mantles throw,
O'er gilded sins—and Death's vain tinsel show,

F

O'er passions, Vice, o'er aught that will uphold,
Your social dignity, or bring you gold ;
Ye are accursed ! with heavier curse than Cain's,
Ye murder souls, the Church's priceless gains !
What can ye plead? your trial is at hand,
And justice hovers o'er the darkened land,—
Awake ! arise ! ere long the trump will sound—
Truth's glorious banner wave thro' all the ground.

Better the days when Ridley's beaming light,
And Latimer's strong beacon glared in sight ;
When Hawkes upreared his burning fingers high
Midst blazing faggots to the far blue sky ;
When lamb - like Cranmer showed his handless
          arm—
Burnt to a cinder—with a smile so calm,
That thousands glorified the power that gave,
To feeble man, a heart so firm and brave.
When myriad saints the long-hid Faith perceived,
And died to prove that which their souls believed ;
Far better 'twere in such a time to live,
Though to the flames our tortured flesh we give,
Than bind our faith to earth with golden chain,
Think we have *all*—though all the world we gain.

          *   *   *   *   *

What matters it—if Rome's dark church maintains,
She holds infallibly Faith's mystic reins—
That *she* alone our consciences may lead,
Prove the true blade—or point the noisome weed?
That Roman Pontiff holds the Keys of Heaven,
That none have Life, save by her blessing given?
What matters it, that England's Church appears
A golden crown upon the failing years?
Or that she pities those whose honest minds
Without her aid Truth's happy presence finds?
What matters if some special sect denies,
That infants unbaptised attain the skies?
Or that another holds that sprinkling saves
Our darling cherubs from eternal graves?
Or that a third believes their Faith is sure,
Who in a church, a chilly bath endure?
What matter if some say, by Grace we're found,
Whilst some, find Grace beneath the Gospel's sound?
That some suppose their own election sure,
Whilst brother saints tormenting doubts endure?
Such notions rise from ill-read histories,
And vain attempts to solve God's mysteries ;
Man may not *all* the Spirit's work explore,
Have Faith, be just, and Heav'n will ask no more !

*　　*　　*　　*　　*

Let Rome pretend—we know her pretence lame,
And others if they choose may know the same—
The living Scriptures are not chained, but free,
Base thought on Truth, then fallacy we see.
If man would know the Truth, plain, undefiled,
He must forget the schools—become a child—
And meekly take the Word as erst 'twas given
From purest fountain in the highest Heaven;
Must cleanse his mind, and then in solemn prayer,
Ask that true light henceforth may linger there;
No man can teach what God alone doth know,
Though doctrines multiply and fancies grow.

Be not deceived, ye hearers of the Word,
The Spirit's teaching e'er must be preferred;
Faith deals with mind, if understood aright—
For things of Heaven are not for present sight;
All forms and ordinances known on earth
Are, outward shadows of an inward birth;
Your fetters drop, away with formal bands,
The soul's vast temple ne'er was made by hands.

The only guide we creatures ere can trust,—
We feeble creatures of to-day and dust,

Is our Creator, whose own Word conveys—
Wisdom to lead us through Life's twilight days—
And loftiest Faith,—to know our heavenly guide,
To trust His power, and in His love abide :
Reveal your Faith by forms, just as you will,
If Christ its author, Peace your souls will fill ;
But trust not Superstition, fancy, show,
By man invented for man's gain below,
For thousands who themselves Christ's followers call,
Are blind Idolaters in Satan's thrall.

        *   *   *   *   *

O come ! bright youth ! attired like fairy Spring,
Robust and joyous, all your treasures bring—
Your bloss'ming hopes, your violets of Love,
O let them spring for nobler things above.
Accept the seeds of Faith's eternal tree,
A glorious plant will rise—its fruit you'll see.

Come ! manhood strong ! like summer's rip'ning sun
Nourish the plant, whose life thy youth begun ;
Its fragrant sprouts, let dews of Prayer attend,
And Showers of Truth will of themselves descend ;
Its spreading branches soon your mind will shield,
And fruits immortal plentifully yield ?

Thrice happy he, who in strong manhood's days,
Walks peacefully Faith's light-enveloped ways !

Come ! mellow age ! like autumn's fields of gold,
Thy waving fruits before the world unfold ;
Thy spring-time's o'er, thy summer's sun hath set,
Thy paling locks with heavy mists are wet ;
Gather Faith's fruit, lay in a plenteous store,
'Twill nourish now, and last for evermore ;
Hold fast the Branch, that bears the ripest load,—
Enjoy the luscious juice upon the road.

Come ! hoary years ! with Winter's crown adorned,
More closely clasp the Branch, by many scorned ;
When chilly winds infirmities increase,
May Faith within, shed beams of warmth and peace ;
The stooping shoulders and the tott'ring gait,
Prove plainly now, you have not long to wait ;
Conscious the River's near, your mind prepare,
Let Faith's bright crown, surmount your snowy hair.
In second childhood—like a child repose,
Life bids thee live, when Death thine eyelids close.

     *   *   *   *   *

O Love adorable ! that leads the mind,
The Understanding trains, true Faith to find ;

To Esau's heel, the hand of Jacob clung—
And Jacob's power in Esau's ear is sung.
Awake ye sleepers—ere Heaven's pleading voice,
Bids darkness fall, and seals your present choice;
The days draw in, ye thoughtless souls attend !
Ere terrors come, for Time must have an end !

ELLEN'S TRIALS.

A Domestic Tale.

TO THE READER.

THINK more of *others'* sorrow,
Then YOURS may lighter seem ;
Hope on to-day—to-morrow
You'll glide thro' smoother stream.

Chapter First.

IS there no Poetry in the haggard cheek—
   The sunken eye, that many sorrows speak—
The anxious gaze—the quick, uneven pace—
The daily sharp'ning of the thoughtful face—
The growing shabbiness of well brushed clothes—
The newly added patches to the hose—
The well-cleaned boots, with heels and soles worn
     down—
The hat still smooth, tho' quickly growing brown—
The clean white shirt—the faded kerchief tied
Ingeniously, a fractured part to hide?
Such signs of wasting, penury, and care,
Unnoticed pass in every city's glare,
But to my mind Thought's fertile stores unfold
Pregnant with wealth more precious than fine gold.
They speak a home, where, round the kitchen grate
Grim Poverty presides in barren state;
But where her power is held in check severe,
By thoughtful tenderness, and words that cheer.

They speak a home, where, tho' the humid eye
Oft fills with tears—tho' heavy hearts oft sigh,
The struggling inmates, blessed by Virtue's smile,
Rest, on sweet Hope, and trust in God the while.
They speak the busy fingers of the wife,
Whose sweet resources ease the chequered life ;
With silent earnestness they seem to say,
" Tho' faded now, we've seen a better day.
Our wearer, oft by inward cares oppressed,
Was once a youth by Fortune's hand caressed,
Was once a youth whom friends were pleased to meet,
And gladly hailed him in the busy street.
Naught then of care his happy brow o'erspread,
His busy hands earned more than daily bread.
But now, tho' at his door no fault doth lie,
His quondam friends unheeding pass him by ;
Some look in pity, and some look with scorn,
On whom misfortune stamps her mark forlorn."

What care the throng, on selfish ends intent,
For virtuous lives, in honest struggling spent ?
The scheming trader, who with busy brain
Works legal frauds, and counts ill-gotten gain ;
The keen-eyed lawyer, rubbing his small hands,
And sideways glancing where his client stands,

With mealy words a doubtful suit prolongs,
Expatiates on his client's rights and wrongs,
Talks him at last into a passive tool,
Draws all he can, then snubs him for a fool.
The gambler, whether if on turf or 'change,
Who proves successful in his ventures strange ;
The lucky jobbers amongst stocks and shares,
The tricky vendors of a thousand wares,
The harden'd publican, to Satan wed,
Who gilds his vaults to snare the living dead ;
To these, and such as these, respect is shown,
They're monied men, and therefore, are well known ;
Are praised and courted, and held up to view
As men of worth, industrious and true.

  O give me, rather, Poverty and want,
Let worldly comforts meagre be and scant ;
If to my heart unerring Wisdom says,
Such fruits they reap who follow Virtue's ways,
And tho' the crowd so lapt in pride and show,
Still after vice in painted garments go,
With tearful glance, I pity, yet despise,
Their honours here, may ours be in the skies.

*   *   *   *   *

Farewell awhile, ye sunny purling streams,
Whose glossy wavelets glow with purpling beams ;

Ye verdant fields who nurse the flowers wild—
Thou springing lark, sweet Harmony's own child.
Ye cornfields, bending 'neath the fragrant breeze ;
Ye flow'ry brambles, and ye spreading trees,
Ye glorious wastes of purple and of gold,
Ye plashing waterfalls and headlands bold,
Ye sylvan nooks, in fancy-stirring dell—
Ye lonely walks, awhile—awhile farewell ;
No fragrant breezes waft their perfume here,
On every side tall warehouses appear ;
With gloomy walls dark frowning on the street,
Where sweating teams in rough confusion meet—
Where blust'ring carters with impatience burn,
Use language foul and quarrel 'bout their " turn."
From giddy heights the dangling ropes descend,
The swinging bales their upward courses wend—
And high the brawny porters fearless stand,
At open doors with ready hooks in hand,
Strike as they come the bulky pond'rous bales,
Which trembling stop, then fall beside the scales.

The street is narrow—the atmosphere thick—
The sickly sun shines on the dusty brick ;
The unemployed are wand'ring to and fro,
Or leaning 'gainst a pothouse mean and low.

Fatigue in every face attests its power,
For double work have they who spend the lazy
    hour.

Sweet noontide now is quickly drawing near,
Its welcome chimes fall on the waiting ear.
Still hang the ropes, the folding doors unite—
Each spiral staircase, dark as winter's night,
With tread resounds of numerous heavy feet,
All hast'ning to the dust-encumbered street.

Soon all is still, save where at yonder gate
Three women, talking, for their husbands wait.
Each carries in her hand the mid-day meal,
In well-wrapped cans, which oftentimes they feel,
And murmur—wond'ring at the strange delay—
" The dinners surely will be cold to-day."
But now the partly opened gate swings wide,
The women cease to murmur—stand aside ;
Draw near the men with solemn nod or smile,
Bid them to wait—their hearts beat hard awhile,
For on their husbands' shoulders softly borne,
Bleeding and wan, of strength and feeling shorn,
A young man rests, with partly opened eyes,
Sightless and dull fixed on the burning skies.

A fractured limb is held by one rough hand,
Is gently held—while close the women stand—

Their cans forgotten as they breathe their fears,
Or turn to hide the sympathetic tears ;
Till one unbidden hastened up the street—
Thinking, perchance, a passing car to meet,
Nor disappointed, found one rumbling by,
And gesturing hail'd it with a loud hie ! hie !
Its course now turned, she points and leads the way,
To where the porters with their burden stay ;
And here she heard the story simply told,
Of how a bale had from a high pile rolled—
Struck, as it fell, the clerk on work intent,
As o'er a weight-book thoughtfully he bent.

Chapter Second.

HOW sweet and sacred the experience,
    Mingling with solid joy our every sense,
Of home love and of calm domestic bliss.
But Oh ! what thousands these fond blessings miss.
    The distant trav'ler wand'ring far from home,
Sighing, will listen to the wind's dull moan,
As thro' his mind, soft thoughts will creep apace,
Subdue to tears his weather-beaten face.
The pleasant fireside rises to his view,
He sees the glowing embers' crimson hue ;
His mother's features, ruddy in their light
Smile, as she pats his sunny locks so bright.
The steaming urn the welcome hot tea pours,
His sister prattling creeps upon all fours,
And once again sweet happy faces gleam,
And once again he glories in their beam ;
The wilderness or flood he now doth roam,
Seems changed, O happy change, for childhood's home.
    Domestic bliss—such bliss as parents know,
When cherub faces round their table glow;

H

Ere icy Death or Want's stern hand appears,
To drown their happiness in blinding tears,
Thus far had been fair Ellen's happy lot—
Love *lodged* not only in her humble cot,
But lived presiding Genius of the place,
And lit with pleasant smiles each charming face.   •

  A pretty cottage, Ellen's, scarcely seen
For shading elms and ivy's darker green ;
At front a grass plot neatly hedged around,
Small — but so smooth and close, the verdant
      ground
Seems like a carpet of soft velvet pile,
For fairies spread 'neath beauty's sweetest smile.
Inside the hedge a flowery border blooms,
Wafts its sweet perfume thro' the neighb'ring rooms,
Than which no places could more clean and neat,
Be made for tread of snowy angels' feet.
And angels dwelt there, two sweet cherubs fair,
Fond Ellen's pride—her husband's joy and care.
Like dress'd-up dolls they stumbled to and fro,
Their mirth unchecked, all unrestrained its flow.

  Alas ! poor Ellen, as to thy fond breast,
Each darling babe alternately is pressed ;
Thou little knowest what dark waves of woe
Toward thy sylvan homestead now do flow.

Ere long thy voice, which now so blythe and
    clear
Sings merry lay to please thy infant's ear,
Must change its note—and big with sorrow's freight,
For happy days e'en thou wilt have to wait.

  'Tis evening now—the cabman's shattered fare
For several hours hath lain 'neath Ellen's care ;
Her husband he—so suddenly cut down,
—A weight-clerk to a merchant in the town—
  The injured limb is set—the doctor's gone,
And wet cloths lie the bleeding face upon.
Near to her husband's pillow Ellen leans—
With trembling hand her anxious features screens—
On him, sweet sleep hath laid a soothing hand,
Perchance in strength he walks some bright dream-
    land.
Not so the watcher—cautiously she moves—
Hangs o'er the couch of him she dearly loves ;
As falls the dew upon sear Autumn's dress,
So gently on his brow her kisses press ;
And as the vapours from the warm earth driven,
So mount her noiseless prayers up unto heaven.
O heartfelt prayers are those when none are nigh,
That all unspoken hasten to the sky ;

And oft ere from the trembling heart they've flown,
A peaceful answer starts from His white throne,
Unto whose ear the slightest sigh can speak
Loud as the clarion's far-resounding shriek.

   O Father, would that we could always see
In darkness, or in sunshine, naught but thee ;
Would that we could when sudden trouble tears
Our fondest hopes, replacing them with cares—
Turn unto Thee, our surest Friend and Guide,
Cleave unto Thee, whate'er may us betide,
Breathe unto Thee as silent Ellen breath'd
To find our hearts, like hers, with comfort wreath'd,
For, even now, the anxious looks depart,
Her face bespeaks the gath'ring calmness of her heart.

      *   *   *   *   *

Though weary hang the hours when Pain is nigh—
Tears from the helpless frame the smothered cry—
Strikes the faint nerves with cruel talons strong—
Grim visitant to whom dread powers belong ;
E'en from thy feet, unwelcome child of woe,
Pleasures arise, and flowers of virtue grow.
'Tho' few thy weary vigils care to keep,
Those vigils often end in quiet sleep.
Thy hateful presence, tho' so few can stand,
Oft brings new blessings closer to our hand ;

Love often hides beneath thy blood-stained dress,
And truest beauty 'neath thine ugliness.

   The prostrate body, weakened by thy hand,
Or feebly led on Death's dark shore to stand,
Prepares unconsciously its mental powers
For better days, and brighter, sunnier hours ;
Like as the plough, which in November's days,
Earth's open bosom to the frost displays—
Prepares the crumbling soil for coming spring,
For seed-time, and for summer's ripening.
But O ! 'tis hard when aching pain sits by,
Sweeps balmy sleep from off the upturned eye,
To have such thoughts, and bid the spirit rest,
And bless the hand that probes the feeble breast.
The present evils oft absorb our view,
Our troubled hearts with murmurings imbue.

   Thus 'twas with Ellen's husband when he lay,
Bemoaning the events of that sad day,
Or in the wakeful moments of the night
His dire position flashed before his sight.
Upon his mind, from some mysterious cause,
And unexplainable by settled laws,
Brooding Depression's heavy shadows hung,—
A dread foreboding to his spirits clung ;

The future black, as blackest midnight seemed,
While naught but tenderness around him beamed.
Say, reader, say, hast thou ne'er felt the same?
Canst thou the victim of these broodings blame?
When happiness, and mirth, and hope seem fled,
And—dreadful thought—he wishes he were dead.
Whilst still his dearest blessings round him bloom,
And unchanged love presides within his room.

Whence come those fears,—we've heard the parsons
     say,
"God hides his face, then comes the evil day.
The Deity hath marked some flagrant sin—
Withdrawn his consolation from within,
And left the wretched man alone to fight
The phantoms of his palsied mind and sight."
False teaching this, with earnestness we speak,
False teaching this, cold, mis'rable, and bleak.
Come, turn aside, and view that giddy throng
Which, laughing, trip that brilliant room along;
Or sit, well pleased with every pointless joke
Which mingles with the rising puffs of smoke.
No troubled faces in that gay saloon;
Enjoyment grants her soul-betraying boon;

Mirth sparkles in each dark alluring eye,
The gay walls ring with boist'rous jollity.

The flippant waiters pass with trays around,
And glasses jingling mingle with the sound
Of lively strains, that from a fiddle float,
And noise discordant from a singer's throat.

As towards its close each senseless verse is brought,
The strain is by a fat-faced chairman caught ;
Who, striking a huge desk with hammer small,
Growls—' chorus gentleman,'—uprises all
That motley throng of women and of men,
And murder, with their noise, each dull line o'er
　　　again.
And here for hours they sit, till drink assails
With potent spell, or till their money fails ;
Or till by waiting syren led away.
In other sin to greet the blushing day.

Ah say ! as from the boist'rous scene you turn,
What thoughts within your heaving bosom burn ?
Say, would you choose to join the thoughtless
　　　crowd,
Whose thick'ning voices mingle strong and loud ;
Or bear depression's racking, troubled load
In Virtue's home, and Love's unchanged abode ?

Say, if with it the blessèd hope abides?
Or smiling heaven the gay assembly guides?
 Cheer up, poor sufferer, for thousands know
And dread the shadows thro' which now you go,
A light still beaming shines beyond the gloom,
Love's hand still guides, whate'er thy frail bark's
  doom.

Chapter Third.

"SWEET Zephyrus hail! upon my pallid cheek,
    And wasted frame, thro' close confinement
      weak,
Thy gentle breath comes like refreshing showers
To thirsty soil. in July's sultry hours.
How sweet to feel thy pinions move my hair,
Sweep past my face with fragrance rich and rare,
Expand my lungs with health's reviving stream ;
Sweet Zephyrus hail! and hail, thou yellow beam,
First of thy kindred which hath kissed my brow
For many weeks; I greet thee, love thee, now,
As when in childhood's hours I stole from home,
In daisied fields, and brambly woods to roam."

Thus spake the clerk, in contemplation lost,
As each soft breeze his humid forehead crossed.
So low he spake, his accents scarce can reach
This shading Elm, or silv'ry line of Beech ;
But yet the murm'ring caught the quickened ear
Of gentle Ellen, ling'ring wistful near.

I

Light as a fawn, close to his side she skips,
Bends her fair neck and meets his upturned lips.

"Yes! dearest husband! from the sick-room free,
How sweet to sit beneath our old elm-tree;
How sweet to hear the breeze's plaintive sigh—
To watch the silv'ry vapours of the sky,
To feel the sun's warm, ever-welcome ray,
Reanimate this frail and wasted clay.
Health greets you now, the dreadful danger's past,
O let your mind no more be overcast.
The same kind Providence, whose guiding hand
Leads yon bright swallows from each wintry land,
Hath led you thro' each anxious day of pain—
Healing and Peace hath brought to us again.
With meek and thankful hearts let us adore—
Whom our complaints with gentle pity bore."

"Heav'n has been good to us, dear wife, and
        kind,
But churlish fancies still molest my mind.
Few are the hours when calm content or joy,
Rest on my soul, unmixed with gloom's alloy;
'Tho' health return, I feel 'tis not decreed
From influence malign I should be freed.

Why should I look for peace where none is
    known?
The changeful world in which our lot is thrown
Might possibly show one eternal round
Of quietness, nor pride nor hate be found,
Nor wild ambition on her blood-stained wings,
Nor avarice whose dirt to millions clings.
But ere that time may come, all change must cease;
'Tis change destroys our every hope of peace.
And love of change seems now our one desire—
Where'er we are, we wish ourselves much higher—
Whate'er we be, whate'er our present state,
Or rich, or poor, ignoble, learned, or great,
Our restless spirits still within us burn,
For this—for that—and everything in turn.
Society and fashion fan the flame,—
They're change itself in everything but name.
Look carefully around our circle small,
Take friends, acquaintances, relations all,
O what a jostling in their midst appears—
What wicked tales are told to willing ears;
What jealousies and pettyfogging pride,
And restless longings in their midst abide;
What senseless quarrels, broached without a cause,
What signs of rage, what paltry paper wars,

What cold looks rest upon a once loved face,
What angry glances one another chase
From eyes where erst sweet sympathy abode,
And love, by springing tears, her presence showed.

What means all this?—it certainly is strange,
To say the cause of all is wish for change.
And yet it seems so.—Cousin Bob, a clerk
In that great firm of lawyers, Gripe and Shark,
Fumes o'er his books and marks with envious
    eye
His master's dapper pony-chaise pass by.
With stern resolve o'er legal authors pours—
Even his playful children he terms 'bores,'
If they disturb the sober, stately train
Of learnèd thoughts that pass into his brain.
He'll fight his way, he says, a change there'll be,
Bob in his carriage some fine day we'll see.
But in the meantime, Bob's whole life is sad—
His wife, too, says his temper's very bad.

Then Bob's fine master, owner of the chaise,
Doth he find peace the crown of prosperous days?
Ah, no! he too must change the daily round
Of dull routine within his office found.
The borough wants a member—and his friends,
To suit their interests, he to suit his ends,

Proclaim his name on flaming placards red,
Their chosen candidate—the very dead
Might groan in startled anger at the noise,
The yells, the cheers from women, men, and boys,
Which on election day attend the fight,
The contest fierce from morn to closing night.
His mind exultant—thinks not of defeat—
'"Tis four o'clock,' he cries, ' I've gained the seat !'

One now might think contentment's placid smile
Would to her realms his restless soul beguile.
Vain thought! new visions now his mind expand,
On greater heights he thinks ere long to stand.
That which is reached, but shows how small he was,
When courting friends or stupid mobs applause.

'Tis here that education seems at fault,
'Tis hers this frenzied feeling to assault,
But e'en her influence benign is made,
A tool of strife—a handle to its blade.
But come, dear Ellen, with me to the gate,
Surely the Postman is this evening late :
I need not say from whom 'tis time to hear,
A crisp bank-note my heart perchance may cheer."

" Say not, dear husband, that in cash consists
The cheering of the heart ; the gloomy mists

And shadows fanciful, that have depressed,
Chase them, for ever, from your honest breast;
No more by them a willing slave be made,
From Love's endearments be no more betrayed;
Then may a change, we all desire, take place,
And beaming smiles light up a darling face.
But see! adown yon grassy belt of road,
The civil Postman hastens with his load;
Hither he comes! perhaps dark Fate now grants
The crispy boon, for which your bosom pants."

A melancholy smile a moment played
Upon his features, then away it strayed,
Sudden and sickly, like a faint moonbeam
Struggling through clouds to kiss some shaded stream,
And thus he answer'd—"Little 'tis I care
Whether my purse be full or pocket bare;
'Tis for thy sake, dear Ellen, and for theirs
Who sleep in rosy innocence upstairs—
Our darling babes, their future life, and thine,
Around my heart, what fears, what hopes, entwine?
For well I know the bleakness of the world
When Poverty hath once her flag unfurl'd."
But here he is, and there the letter lies;
Ah! watch his features, mark his sad surprise,

As o'er each line the pale-blue note contains,
With gloomy interest his dark eye strains.
No crispy note, no welcome cheque is there—
The more he reads, the greater his despair.
The firm has failed, the partners too have flown,
O'er all the town the news ere then was known.
Nothing is left—naught e'en the clerks to pay,
Nor hope of aught on any future day.

Fond Ellen, ling'ring near the shaded seat,
Saw disappointment in his face. With sweet
Consoling words she bade him rise and come
Into their pleasant, comfortable home.
And when she knew the worst, around his neck
She flung her arms and kissed him. "Fear no wreck
Of happiness or home," she cheering said ;
"Remember how five thousand men were fed.
Though for the present your employment's gone,
Another clerkship may ere long be won.
No one can your fair character assail,
And other firms there are, though this one fail."

"Ah, dearest ! would that I on Hope's bright wing
Could mount like you, and wished-for blessings bring
So near that they upon our present plight
Might shed one ray of soul-reviving light.

But 'tis not so—my heart's of sadder mould,
Here melancholy's train their griefs unfold.
Even in prosp'rous days her horrid shade
Will haunt me, and my inmost soul invade.
But now, with these reverses on my mind,
I dread the future as oft-hunted hind
Might dread the distant baying of the hounds,
When timid fawn beside her nimbly bounds;
She knows what those dread sounds portend,
    and I
Know more than you of this town's misery.
Fain would I hope, but ah! I know how small
The chance is here to get a place at all.
When one is vacant, soon the lists are filled
By stern competitors well backed and drilled;
Each by experience got in former fights
A mealy application note indites,
In bold hand, writ with unaccustomed pains,
Careful and clear, free from all blots and stains.
Enclosed are testimonials three or four,
Or references from one to half a score,
To first-class merchants, all well known on 'Change
(A phrase to poor outsiders passing strange).
Ah! what a tale these well-penned letters tell,
As one by one the rising pile they swell.

Hundreds unopened lie the desk beside,
And hundreds opened fill a basket wide.
How can the advertiser hope to choose
One in a thousand, and the rest refuse?
In sheer despair, the mighty task he leaves,
And some known clerk the vacant place receives.
And thus a thousand writers write in vain,
A thousand writers wait to write again.
And how can I, weakly, depressed, and sore,
Expect to find some ready-opened door,
Whilst others good as me, both young and old,
Stand waiting, shiv'ring in misfortune's cold?"

K

Chapter Fourth.

SUMMER has gone — beneath the cold grey skies—
The bleak wind whistles, and the snowdrift lies.
A warmer clime the graceful Swallows found,
The late green leaves lie bleaching on the ground.
The Finch has left the woodlands' leafless bower,
The Bee no longer seeks the blighted flower.
From lone retreat the fearless Robin comes,
Chirps at the window for the welcome crumbs ;
The wild ducks wander inland for their food,
The mother hen protects her late-hatched brood ;
And as the early ev'nings close apace,
To cheerful fire comes many a blue cold face.
Down fall the blinds—the brilliant curtains close,
Thro' many a chink the inside brightness glows.

But how is this? fair Ellen's cot remains
Cheerless and dull,—the frosty window-panes
Still hold their magic tracery up to sight—
Sparkling and beautiful i' the cold moonlight.

Hast thou, sweet Ellen, like the swallows flown
To some bright land, more genial than thine own?
Thy cherub infants dost thou now caress,
Where summer waves in radiant loveliness?
Alas! 'tis vain to ask, we've heard her tale
Sighed by the pitying breeze along the vale.
We know how disappointments pressed her down,
Where now she dwells in yonder busy town;
How one by one her treasured household things
Fled,—charmed away on Poverty's black wings;
How those who should her closest friends have
    stood,
Heedless of friendship or the ties of blood,
Left her alone,—or coming only spoke
With railing words, and added to the stroke;
And how her bruisèd spirit, hopeful still,
With resignation strove to meet each ill;
How o'er her Husband's mind, gloom held its sway,
With gath'ring darkness each despair-crowned day.
More than aught else, this troubled Ellen's mind;
Than loss of home—or Fortune's frowns unkind.
Her wretched lodging, with its scanty store,
Might yet be changed, and bright as heretofore.
But slowly dying that fond hope appeared,
As there he sat—by trouble more endeared—

Speechless and sad—with dull and vacant stare,
On floor carpetless, and window bare.
And fearful thoughts the starting tears restrain,—
O God ! these frightful cares may overcome his brain !

'Twas in December, from the bleak north-east,
The with'ring wind pierced thro' both man and beast ;
The mocking sun, athwart the waking town,
Shot slanting rays of heatless amber down.
Poor Ellen's husband left their wretched place
To breast the cold—his pinched and haggard face
Well corresponded with his scanty dress,
Much worn, but yet arranged with carefulness.
A staff was in his hand, from which he found
Relief when on the hard uneven ground
His still weak foot was placed.　Upon this morn,
So cold and bleak, he looked the more forlorn,
Staring about with sharp inquiring gaze,
Like some late-risen shade of other days.
The town lay south, but careless where he went,
Towards the north his wand'ring footsteps bent.
Anon he turned and trembled as he walked,
As if some spectre by the wayside stalked ;
Then with incoherent mutt'rings sped along,
Or murmured snatches of some doleful song.

Until at length the streets are left behind,
And naked trees creak in the wintry wind ;
Upon the right an open country lies,
And on the left the restless billows rise.
And here he sat upon a shell-strewn rock,
Regardless of the bleak wind's searching shock.
Floated sublime the grey clouds overhead,
Strong on the wing the sweeping sea-birds sped ;
With myriad hoary feelers of bright foam,
Old Ocean crept from out his caverned home.
Here stout star-grass before wild Boreas bent,
Lifelike upstarting e'er his power was spent ;
There speckled sea-pairs twittered on the sand,
Whilst cawing rooks came from their home inland.
Unseen by him the gathering waters rose,
In spreading arms the shingly rock enclose,
Unnoticed, passed the stately sails to sea,
Unheard, the thrush sang on the sloping lea.

A death-like stupor o'er his senses steals—
He neither sees — nor hears — nor thinks — nor
        feels ;
Whilst slowly rising from his caverns deep,
The hoary monarch o'er the sand doth creep,
Sprinkling with foam his cold unconscious feet.

At length the staff falls from his nerveless hand,
Floats on the wavelets to the bending strand,—
And list ! high borne upon the sweeping gale,
Comes from the shore a wild heart-rending wail.
Liked some tired elk, by wary sportsman found,
And pierced by shot, leaps startled from the ground,
Only to fall again a helpless mass,
Wounded and writhing on the purpling grass ;—
So leaped the clerk, released from deathlike spell—
Then on the rock, bewildered, helpless, fell ;
And tho' no purple stream the shingles dyed,
Benumbed and sore he lay amidst the tide.
Surprise and fear had drawn that startling cry
From faithful Ellen as she hastened by—
(Induced by inward fears for him to seek,
So wan and worn, so troubled and so weak) :
She'd marked the course his heedless footsteps took
With anxious sigh and timid fearsome look.
" Why do you take," she thought, " that northward
      track ?
I'll go, dear husband, bring you safely back."
With searching gaze she'd wandered to the shore,—
Carefully scanned each frozen sand-hill o'er,
Until at length his drooping form she spied
Surrounded by the rising waters wide.

No second sound, save that of indrawn breath,
Escaped her ; pale and motionless as death,
Or as some statue carved by cunning hand,
Or as some nymph forlorn cast on the sand,
She stood ; but O how changed that sweet face now,
Since 'neath the Elms she kissed her infant's brow.
Then, comfort's hand a downy mantle spread,
And blooming Health tinged each bright cheek with
     red ;
Now are discerned thro' pale transparent skin
The fine blue veins meandering within.
Gone are the roses living there for years,
Gone, washed away by oft-recurrent tears ;
But like the pink-streaked shells that round her lay,
Tho' she grew thin, she grew more beautiful each
     day.

But half recovered from the stup'rous sleep,
The clerk, bewildered, gazed upon the deep ;
His gentle wife, he saw on surgy brink,
With foot advanced, as tho' she would not shrink
To pass the watery barrier, that moved,
Between the shore, and him she fondly loved.
  The long-pent tears from dreamy eyes diffuse,
A sudden strength his feeble frame renews,

And, cheerily, he bade her wait awhile,
And waved his hand, with old, accustomed smile;
"No serious depth," he cried, "of water's here;
The tide has turned, and soon 'twill all be clear."

"The tide has turned,"—was that what he had said?
"The tide has turned,"—kept ringing thro' her head.
And was that his—her gloomy husband's hand
Waving that sweet assurance unto land?
"Thank heav'n," she said; "thank heav'n for that
      changed tone,
Come, husband! come! I am no more alone."

     *   *   *   *   *

And hath thy tide of trouble turned, fond wife?
Doth comfort's sunshine now make glad thy life?
Hath thy firm Faith its sure reward received,
Hath active Love thy weary days relieved?
  With lighter step she hastens up the stair,
With lighter heart, a busy husband's there—
Her children, too, are warmly clad, and well,
New odds and ends her meagre treasures swell;
And tho' her husband's income's very small,
Yet, she contrives not quite to part with all;
Sometimes, with happy face, to him she showed
The earnings which from her own labours flowed;

Then would he chide her, for her secret pains,
But she would laugh and put away the gains;
And thus their days, in work and peace, were spent.
He, saved by her, now blessed with rich content.

    *   *   *   *   *

Ye merchant *Princes*, ye, to whose bright homes
The chilling shade of Penury ne'er comes;
Think more of those whose aching heads and hands
Improve your trade in this and foreign lands;
Dole not their pittance with a miser's eye,—
Feel for their wants and prove your sympathy.
If ye assume the name, accept the part,
Act with a noble, generous, *princely* heart.

YOUTH AND AGE;

OR,

THOUGHTS ON THE PRESENT STATE OF RELIGION, MORALITY, AND EDUCATION.

——o——

𝔓art 𝔉irst.

" Thou whose sweet youth and early hopes inhance
Thy rate and price, and mark thee for a treasure,
Hearken unto a Verser, who may chance
Ryme thee to good, and make a bait of pleasure :
A verse may finde him who a sermon flies,
And turn delight into a sacrifice."

—GEORGE HERBERT.

Part First.

" DREAM on, great Land—dream on in peaceful
  sleep,
Men now no longer watch, nor women weep ;
No baleful fires light up the distant hill,
No painful shrieks the ambient air now fill ;—
No victims doomed to die on fiery pile,
To writhe in anguish, 'neath the sick'ning smile
Of monkish hypocrites, who stand around
And hear with hellish glee each torturous sound,
Who mark the head droop on the burning breast,
With fiendish joy—with laughter unrepressed.
Security and Peace seem now to reign,
Our fair land cleansed from bigotry's red stain.
Love seems to show her bright unsullied face,
And knowledge every happy home to grace ;
The public mind to learn and ponder well,
Ungarnished Truth for which our fathers fell :—
For which our mothers braved the stake and flame,
With godlike zeal to Death or torture came.
Wherefore this change ? why all so quiet now ?
Is heavenly Love stamped on each thoughtful brow?

Doth sweet Religion shed her holy beams—
Pour o'er the land her pure empyreal streams ?
Ah no ! Religion's light is dim and sad,
Her smile makes not the passive people glad ;
O look with care around—how few the breasts
Where her sweet hope or sacred influence rests—
Form and display on every hand are spread,
True Faith lies languishing and well-nigh dead,
Mechanical routine lulls most to sleep,
And dry formalities no watches keep.

   Men stand and preach throughout the live-long
      day,
But preaching's talk—they act not as they say—
They teach humility—but practise pride,
Look scornful round them, and with pompous stride,
Pass by their hearers, who with toil-stained hands
Direct the plough or till the fallow lands.
They preach and say how dreadful is the stain
Cast o'er the Christian's life by love of gain,—
But slyly gather all the wealth they can,
In secret venerate the monied man.

   Now the great pride of Christian Teachers seems
To be in mighty edifice, that beams
With architectural beauty, and that rears
High its proud head above men's graves and biers—

In chiming bells, whose sweet-toned music swells
Throughout the city where the poor man dwells.
Each silvery no e may mock an aching heart,
Pierced by misfortune's unrelenting dart.
The sacred Church renowned thro' every age—
Guardian of Life, upreared on holy page—
A good man there should hold an honoured post,
A righteous man rank high in God's own host ;
Truth there with Love should flourish—Virtue, shine,
And Joy, and Peace, and Equity combine
To show the world that God is held supreme,
That Faith is real—no sentimental dream.

    But do those silvery bells' delightful tone,
To man's tried heart make such a sweet place
       known ?
A joyful chord touch in the sinner's breast,
Inviting him to come—believe—be blest ?
Or by their chiming do they only say,
"Come hear a sermon—or, come see a play,
Come, clothe yourselves in gorgeous raiments fine,
Your neighbour's elegance you must outshine :
Come say your prayers, and have your sins forgiven ?"

    By whom ? by men who know, nor God, nor Heaven,
Except perchance by hearsay or by rote,
Which knowledge they impart from drawling throat.

Whose hearts are hard—whose practice teaches
    naught,
Except to give the lie to doctrines taught
By word of mouth,—here consciences are eased,
And rich men's vanities and fancies pleased—
Here lettered tablets on the wall proclaim
The brilliant virtues of some noble name,
Acknowledged after its possessor's death,
But never known whilst he drew mortal breath.

  'Tis here that thoughtful men are asked to pray,
To worship God upon His holy day.
To these Divines the ear must open wide,
The soul must take them as its surest guide ;
The mind must ponder all their words with care,
And well digest the food their hands prepare.

  Presumptuous man, you say, thus to assail
Our gentle curate,—call our Parson frail !
Our well-loved Pastor, whose uplifted hand,'
Is ready ere at Charity's demand
To give his mite, and bless the hungry poor
Who gather daily round his dwelling's door.

  Watch closer, ye who love Religion's name,
Ye who are jealous of her spotless fame,—
Then mark the Pride, the love of World you'll find
Within your so-called gen'rous Parson's mind.

O ! what a thinning of their ranks you'd see,
If Mammon gilded not their Piety.
But go, your saintly Parsons go to hear,
Whilst I pursue my walk o'er pastures dear
Unto my memory—where oft I've lain,
On summer's Eve, to mark the glowing plain
Receive day's parting beauties—fading fast—
And sadly grieve to see how soon they'd past."

Thus (walking) mused a Youth o'er whose fair head,
Some twenty summers had their richness spread ;
His way led him to the waving fields,
Whose broad expanse man's chief subsistence yields ;
All here was calm, the heavy lazy breeze
In quiet rested in the neighbouring trees ;
But now and then would sigh, then creep along
And murmur thro' the wheat its softest song ;
Bending the hanging ears in playful strife
As if their richness had renewed its life.
  The young man stood and gazed upon the scene,
And blessed the yellow corn, the pasture's smiling green.
Above—a cloud sailed in the ruddy west,
In changing colours beautifully drest.
He thought it like the quickly passing years,
Now bright with hope, now dull with thronging fears ;

M

But as it moved 'twas by a sidewind caught,
Dissolved its beauty—its smooth course cut short.
And thus he spoke :—" What art thou, Life, but
breath,
Dispersed at once by unrelenting Death ?
His icy breathings paralyse the frame,
Chill the warm blood—put out the flick'ring flame.
The passive body yields its clammy pores,—
The silent soul withdraws thro' unhinged doors.'
But where when from the stricken body fled
Goes the mysterious essence ? 'midst the dead
It cannot rest, for 'tis the breath of God,
Which never slumbers 'neath an earthly sod.

'God breathed into the man, and he became
A living soul.' It must be still the same,
Each human creature moulded from the earth
Must have received his holy breath at birth.—
So each must once have been both pure and good,
As Adam was in manly babyhood.—
And then we pass our hazy childhood's years,
When pleasures mingle with our unfelt tears,
And each the same to us—we know not why
We laugh and clap our hands, or weep and cry,—
We scarcely know we live, till Reason's eyes
Dimly discern, and thoughts just noticed rise.

Then, soon by natural instinct taught, we find,
Those who to us are loving, good, and kind ;
And cling to them, and nestle in their breast,
Finding new joy in being there at rest.

Then as our opening faculties expand,
We look for food from mother's gentle hand,
And watch her face, there soon perchance to see
The change from joy to dull anxiety.
We are too young to understand this change,
Yet wonder why it comes, and think it strange.
Our childish hearts with mystic feeling swell ;
We know, when fond ones weep, all is not well.

But with sweet childhood's years away hath
flown
All innocence that in the world is known ;
Passions arise, and soon our wilful tongue
Repeats untruths, and things we know are wrong.
Hate and Deceit begin their troubled reign,
And Purity's defiled with Sin's dark stain.
Ere we can know the consequence of sin,
We have committed it, and are within
Its damnèd circle, living 'neath the curse
Of Him who made us—and what is still worse,
Tho' Death may come, no fond relief he brings,
The curse to us thro' endless ages clings.

O ! it is fearful thus to muse and think !
If this be true, what myriads on the brink
Of yawning gulf do stand—from which arise
Gnashings and groans which mock the placid skies.

    Ye careless shepherds of the starving sheep,
If this be true, O why do you not weep?
Why trust to dead mechanical display,
When dying men lie gasping all the day !
If this be true——"

                    " Who asks if this be true ? "

    " I ask it, grey-haired man ; and who are you
That silent steps from out the twilight's shade ? "

    " I am a man ripe for the still sharp blade
Of old Time's sickle—what art thou, vain Youth,
To question thus the heav'n-writ line of truth ?
Why ask thyself ' if this be true ? ' go, seek,
Search thro' the holy page with spirit meek—
No ' ifs ' will then your wav'ring mind assail,—
For earnest searchers God withdraws the veil.
Eternal Love enshrines Almighty power,
See them combined in Calvary's dark hour,
And let that scene all gathering doubts dispel—
Christ ne'er had died were there no Heaven, or Hell.
Once learn to doubt—then doubts will grow apace,
Delay or stem the stream of heav'nly grace."

" Desist, old man ; thy eyes with fiery roll,
I feel, can penetrate my inmost soul.
And let me ask, why hast thou stepped aside
From thy lone walk, my musings thus to chide ?
Alone I've wandered from the city's noise
To taste the sweets of silent rural joys.
I love to hear the bird's sweet evening hymn,
And watch the blue and rosy sky grow dim ;
The stillness puts my ruffled mind in tune,
And I can here all undisturbed commune
With my own heart—but, unperceived, you heard
The thoughts expressed, that have my bosom stirred ;
And now you sternly lecture me because
I ponder, wondering, over moral laws—
Yet if I err, and tho' thy speech be stern,
I'll listen meekly, and thus strive to learn."

 " Young man, my old heart yearns to set thee right,
And much I'm grieved to hear thy speech to-night.
The words you erewhile uttered seem to me
To be inspired by our arch enemy.
He is permitted every soul to test,
And snake-like worms himself in each young breast.
 To some he flatt'ring speaks with sweetened
 guile—
With honied words and almost angel's smile ;

Whispers loud praises in their willing ears,
Extols their virtues and subdues their fears.
Always unto their minds, their good works showing—
Their public prayers, their alms, or their church-
    going.
Their moral life, apparently so pure,
Will, so he whispers, their shortcomings cure ;
And sometimes, oft at Satan's instigation,
A church they build to crown their reputation."

  "That's what I think !" the youth in rapture cried.
"Hold ! do not interrupt," the seer replied.
"Such works are good, and worthy of renown,
Tho' of themselves they merit not the crown ;
'God loves a cheerful giver,' but He must
With gifts and works, have meekness, child-like
    trust,
And holy faith in the one atonement made,
If man would live, nor be of Death afraid.
But these chief features in the desperate case,
The evil one would banish from their place ;
And so by substituting moral pride
Man's utter helplessness he fain would hide ;
For trusting in oneself he knows full well
To be the surest path that leads to hell.

Within the fold the Tempter often finds
Some tender Lambs of timid, fearsome minds;
Who falt'ring lean against the chilly walls,
And doubting listen while the Shepherd calls.
His gentle voice and promises so dear,
So well adapted both to soothe and cheer,
The enemy would drown with thund'rings great
Of broken laws—of early sins and late,
Of wicked thoughts indulged, vile deeds committed,
Until the victim cries—'I am not fitted
God's spotless purity to share or see,
He calls, but O! He never calls to me!
Yet while he cries, with cold drops on his brow,
No saint ere safer stood, than he stands now.
His cry of agony the shepherd hears,
Strengthens his Faith, and thus subdues his fears;
And tho' the Tempter, foiled, renew the strife,
The weakness of the Lamb oft proves the life.

Others about the fold, the Tempter brings
To grief and trouble by vain reasonings.
Those whom he finds with powers of mind en-
    dowed,
Above the common herd, or motley crowd,
He keenly watches, till the poisoned dart
Of disputatious pride puffs up the heart;

The vain mind then, backed up by Satan's wiles,
At Truth revealed contemptuously smiles ;
Pretends to prove that it cannot agree
With nature's laws, which every day we see—
Measures with Deity its puny arm,
And 'midst disciples weak works untold harm.

Watch, ever watch, the secret works within
For in the *heart* bad actions all begin ;
Nip proud and sceptic thoughts in very birth,
Ere their vile fruits are scattered o'er the earth.

Watch like the swordsman, who, with keen point
        high,
Marks well the foeman's sternly roving eye,
Nor sees the tightened grip, the glitt'ring blade.
Knowing the stroke is by the eye first made,
He whirls his flashing weapon to o'erthrow
The Foe's intent, ere falls the threatened blow.

Others again he tempts, by pointing out
The foibles of their neighbours round about ;
Choosing from those who loudly do profess
To wear religion's charitable dress—
Who regularly go, upon God's day,
With solemn face, to listen and to pray.
A deacon, may be, who does all things well
In church and sunday-school, and doth excel

In stately bows to rich, slight nods to poor—
Varying with the sum dropt at the door,
But whose life tends full six days out of seven
Towards dark Hades rather than to Heaven.

At such an one the thoughtless, pointing, say
' Religion's not a thing for every day ;
'Tis but a cloak the sneaking wretches wear
To blind the people whom they fleece and tear.'
But granting that base hypocrites abound,
That all our neighbours in their ranks be found ;
Yea, granting priests ordained join the mean
        throng,
No reason this we should to it belong :
A reason this that we should rather grieve,
Nor quibbling talk, nor mocking disbelieve.
As well might men who labour in dark mines,
Where sickly lamps give all the light that shines,
Deny the radiant sun that glows above—
The fresh'ning breeze—the leafy waving grove,
Because, forsooth, no sun shines where they be,
No fresh breeze fans—no waving groves they see.

Oh, if some choose to travel in a path
Dark with the threat'nings of eternal wrath,
Be yours and mine to steadily progress,
Illumined by the Sun of Righteousness :

                         N

Be yours and mine to show well as we can
The true, safe road unto the erring man,
Nor dare in pride our fellow-worm despise ;
We're sinful all till we attain the skies.
Oh, let our actions, based on Truth divine,
With love to God and fellow-sinners shine ;
Nor let us from His tabernacle stay,
Nor wander, murm'ring, on His chosen day,
Though half the congregation and the priest
To travel heavenward have long since ceased."

    " But can I not beneath this outstretched dome
Worship full well as if at church or home ? "

    " The heart renewed can worship everywhere,
Whether in prisons dark or cornfields fair,
Or in the curtained bed which sickness shrouds,
Or in the open, 'neath the sailing clouds.
But what if each should wander forth alone,
Nor ever meet around the Father's throne,
How could the flock that plain command fulfil,
Or how obey the Shepherd's written will ?
    " ' Gather ye yourselves together ' was His word,
Whose power with life sepulchred bodies stirred.
With that command He gave the promise sweet
To sit and guide where'er His people meet.

The feast's prepared, His snow-white table's spread,
He sits benignly, breaks the holy bread ;
Oh, then, draw near, nor vacant leave your place,
Draw near for strength, for guidance, and for grace."

The old man paused—His hearer, waiting, stood
With fair cheek redden'd by the mantling blood.
Around, thick gath'ring clouds with roseate hue
Still fringed, replaced the mellow evening's blue.
And one by one, upon the meadow's breast,
The trilling larks dropt to their dewy nest.
And one by one the parting beams expire,—
The shadowy denizens of air retire ;
Till grey and ghost-like, in the shade arise
Columns of mist, and float into the skies.

" Night falls apace ; thou ancient man, O come,
Let me conduct thee to thy hallowed home ;
For hallowed must that place for ever be,
Which shelters Age and earnest Piety."

Part Second.

Part Second.

IN earnest thought, the youth had passed the night,
    Yet morning's beams found him both fresh and
        bright—
No haggard mien, tho' on his now pale cheek,
Could be discerned the unwiped teary streak.
He hailed the light with joyous heart, and went
Again to him, with whom the eve was spent.
  The old man, up betimes, his garden walked,
And Youth and Age, again, together talked.
" Hail, Sire revered ! again I fain would hear
Of themes which to my doubting heart are dear ;
Sincerity I'm sure thou dost possess—
Though seldom found in life's wide wilderness."

  " Why, gentle Youth, such bold assertion make ?
Art thou so old, that thou can'st undertake
To speak thus certainly ? or say how rare
That choicest virtue is on God's earth fair ?
Young life in thee its blossoms scarcely show.
And what of fruit can tender blossoms know ?

Reserve thy judgments till maturer years,
A higher standpost for thy mind uprears;
Seek wisdom earnestly, and you may see,
The world is not so bad as it might be.
    Thy budding soul seems quick and sensitive,
O! shield it, Youth, if thou would'st have it live,
Learn of the violets which in early spring,
Their scented cups to deck the meadows bring;
They nestle low in shielding leaf and grass,
Whilst o'er them ling'ring blasts of winter pass;
How soon would their sweet blossoms droop and die,
Were they to lift their lowly heads on high,
Or strive to emulate the waving flowers
That gild the cheery summer's balmy hours.
As rolling years experiences heap,
Self-confidence grows dim, as after sleep
The wakened mind sees stern realities,
And faints and dies its midnight fantasies."

    "I'm young, 'tis true, and yet my mind appears
As it had lived for many, many years;
From early childhood I my books have loved—
Thro' every class of literature roved.
With teachers oft, and oft with self, I talk;
I read and ponder in each lonely walk.

Earth's giant minds my chief companions are,
To understand their words my constant care ;
And studious youth, now often gathers more
Of learning's fruit and ancient sages' lore,
Than formerly in three-score years and ten,
Could be attained by hard-worked, thinking, men.
For as a stream, by sudden torrents fed,
Soon fills the hollows in its age-washed bed,
And sweeps with giant strides past rock and tree,
To mix with ocean's dread immensity—
So now the Press with books and pamphlets teams,
And young souls float upon the dappled streams,
And pass old rills, with noisy shout and glee,
That slowly trickle to the parent sea."

  " There is some truth, young friend, in what you say,
'Tis true the Press is busy every day—
That Education knocks at every door—
Books take the place of toys on nursery floor ;
But are not untold quires now being soiled,
And ruin's pathway by their influence oiled ?
And so the great broad road is smoother made,
Whilst falt'ring Progress sickens at the trade.
Light flimsy nonsense now seems all the rage,
And booksellers must pander to the age ;

o

True Worth may creeping go, with drooping head,
Its pen scarce brings the hard-earned daily bread.
Tales of foul villany and murders pay,
The veriest trash rolls on its gilded way,
If on the title-page the readers see
The name of some half-crazed celebrity.
'Tis true that Schools arise on every hand,
But ignorance has far from left the land ;
And tho' bright knowledge may in streams rush
    on—
Each clownish parent rear a learnèd son,
O let not favoured intellects pass by,
Or cast on age, though dull, a prideful eye.
The modest rill, which, slowly rippling, flows,
Has time to look about it as it goes ;
Can mark sweet nature's beauties on its way ;
· The feathery fern, the nodding bluebells gay—
The cowslip o'er it sheds its nect'ry dew,
The violet at it peeps, with eye of blue ;
Above its trickling sweet the linnet sings,
Sips on its breast—and cools her sunny wings ;
And when the rill sees opening chasm wide,
Careful it steals adown the rugged side,
Till safely reaching verdant plains below,
Onward again it placidly doth flow—

Its whisp'rings seem for ever to be drowned,
In distant torrents loudly splashing sound—
Or it could oft to proud stream tell a tale,
Of rugged precipice and boisterous gale,
Where mighty waters, broken, fall away,
And hiss, and foam, and rage, in troubled spray.
It often happens those who read the most,
And cram their brain regardless of all cost,
Find that at length a huge chaotic heap—
With useless fragments in their mem'ry sleep.
Always devouring, they can ne'er digest,
Nor choose the food that suits their mind the
        best ;
And thus because each subject they must taste,
Oft strength, and toil, and trouble run to waste ;
As some great pool fed by incessant rains,
Steals o'er its banks and ravages the plains,
The waters doing not the slightest good,
While spreading round their hidden store of mud
Methinks I see some well-known scholars met
Acknowledged truth to burnish or reset ;
Enlightenment presides with knowledge great,
But say, doth Wisdom crown the fair estate?
Why alter language, simple, earnest, plain ;
Perused in youth, in manhood read again?

Each well-known passage—lisped by infant tongue,
—Cherished thro' life our dearest gems among!
What matters if in Hebrew, or in Greek,
Accomplished scholars diligently seek;
Find here a word, or, may be, there a phrase,
Which *they* opine, would better suit our days
By being altered?   If our version shows
The meaning, if the words we have disclose
The hidden sense; if the true spirit's there—
Cease, O ye sages! your great toils forbear!
How can you aid the scholar or the clown,
By dressing Truth in your new-fangled gown?
Travel the road!   Cheer up the fainting
        hosts,
Nor stay to ornament the finger-posts.
Knowledge alone is like a craft at sea,
But Wisdom that craft's pilot ere must be
If it would hope to gain the happy shore—
Nor troubles know, nor doubtings evermore.
O dreadful 'tis the wrecked one's fate to share,
Search in the city, thousands languish there.
See—there is one! you need not wander far,
He leans against the post by yonder car—
The driver he, see how he coughing stands,
The post he clutches with his puffy hands:

His blurred cheek trembles—starts his bloodshot eyes,
With midnight revels twice their proper size.
How mean he looks, in greasy vestments clad,
How dust-begrimed and miserably bad ;
How terrible to hear the wheezing breath
With curses greet the stern inroad of death.
Would'st think that he, whose foul breath taints the
      air,
Whose hollow cough makes passing people stare ;
Whose wat'ry eyes, so dim thro' vice and drink,
And from whose touch the timid children shrink,
Was once a parent's hope, and pride, and joy—
Who struggling laboured for his only boy ?
Was once a student, reading hard to gain
The honours found in Learning's lustrous train ?
    The coveted degree in time he took,
Proud was his heart—proud was his parent's look.
The clever youth had reached the wished-for goal—
Alas ! no anchor held his wayward soul ;
Caressed and flattered, trusting his own power,
No God was thought of in the happy hour.
By friends encircled all things seemed secure—
Pleasures would last and joys for e'er endure.
At length, the wealth by grasping parent earned,
Was by the youth to vicious uses turned ;

And soon the father saw with keen dismay
His life-long hoardings quickly melt away.
But purblind still, with his parental pride,
His son's dark follies from himself would hide.
Excuse his actions—' Youth will have its fling'—
He'll steady soon, and joy and comfort bring.
He's friends above me, men I never knew.
Accomplished, clever, he surely must pull thro'!
Fond, silly man, thy son thou dost but spoil,
Can'st quench a fire by pouring on it oil?
Can'st build a house upon the rolling main?
Will filthy mire wash out a dirty stain?
Life's quicksands spread thy foolish son around,
He slowly sinks—nor feels the solid ground;
The slimy steps of vice he's slipping down,
Will end a vagabond upon the town;
Whilst thou, with aching heart and grey-head bent,
Bemoan thy years almost as much misspent.

Innum'rable the ways, both light and dark,
Where Satan leads, to quench the living spark;
Ten thousand bolts against fair Truth he hurls,
Ten thousand flags of vanity unfurls.
Here, rears a hill of solid, burnished gold,
Where Mammon sits and bids defiance bold;

Where slavish wretches, bowing down, adore,
And lick the dust from off the poisoned floor.
There, guilty Pleasure floats in waves of light,
Allures her victims on to endless night.
Youth, inexperienced, rushes to her arms—
Breathes her lewd breath, and wallows in her
　　charms ;
Nor sees, alas ! within her bosom fair,
Death's fingers grip the hidden dagger there.

　Yet other agencies more potent still
For working woe and ev'ry kind of ill,
Attend on those who in their blindness think
Pleasures to find in strong, insidious drink.

　O Drink ! thou source of misery and dearth,
Curse of the rich—curse of the poor man's hearth—
Top stone of evil—may thy dread reign end—
Chief flower of hell—the devil's staunchest friend.

　For thee the weeping mother sees her store
Of household chattels leave her cottage door ;
She sees her husband with dull, stupid eye,
In empty room, by empty firegrate lie ;
Her shiv'ring children plead aloud for bread,
And one wee thing lifts up the father's head,
Puts it upon her scanty lap to rest,
The flushed face hugging to its infant breast.

Too young to understand—altho' it weeps—
It thinks the father's tired, and only sleeps.

Heaven save thee, mother, in thy cottage bare,
Sweet Hope seems fled, no warm Love lingers there;
Crushed in thy bloom with tender offspring three,
What heart unmoved—thy wretchedness can see—
The haggard victim thou of evil great
Deplored and pampered by each Christian State.
O youth, beware!—for thine own soul beware,
This universal curse, this fearful snare!

On those whose duty 'tis young minds to form—
To train the twigs to best withstand the storm—
To lead them to a haven sweet with rest—
To guide them in the paths of Virtue, blest;
Or they be Parents, Teachers, Guardians, Friends,
What dread responsibility attends.
That little child whose tender, tearful eye
Steals timid glances as you're passing by,
May leave you soon; but years will not efface
Impressions given—thro' manhood one may trace
The good, or ill, effect of slight words spoken,
Quiv'ring o'er the heartstrings till they're broken.
O happy those who meet each little friend,
On golden plains, when troubles have an end;

What joy to see their cherub faces glow,
And think, 'we helped them on their course below;'
What joy to point, with thronging angels near,
To these bright jewels in our life's crown there.
Here is a field where youth or age may sow,
With richness big—with beauty all aglow;
Around on every hand this field is seen
Uncultivated here—here bright and green.
Awaiting blessings fall in genial showers,
Blessed are the workers—blessed the working hours.
And upward springing from the teeming sod,
The sprouting tendrils bless their Maker—GOD.

Ofttimes, when travelling on the narrow road,
When cares oppressed and heavy was our load;
When falt'ring feet slow dragged along the ground,
And Faith in Fear seemed overwhelmed and drowned;
Then sweet the feeling—sweet the solid bliss,
Some fellow-pilgrim's streaming brow to kiss.
Whilst helping him by kindly word or deed,
We found ourselves from weighty burden freed;
And steadily with joy our course pursued,
Our hearts enlarged, our failing strength renewed.
To troubled saints the gentle shepherd shows
A hundred ways whereby to seek repose—

P

A hundred ways diverse, tho' each one tends
To further here the great Eternal's ends ;
Which are, as by the wide creation proved,
Summ'd up in this, 'to love and to be loved.'"

And thus the youth with doubtful air replied,
"Such earnest thoughts shall in my heart abide.
But O ! how easy 'tis old laws to quote,
And hackney'd virtues, thus to mark and note ;
How easy 'tis in solemn tone to say,—
'Who love their fellows God's known will obey.'
Go ! tell the sparrow how the skylark sings,
Fanning the upper air with sunny wings ;
Go ! tell the bat, the noble eagle flies
From lofy eyric, thro' the vaulted skies.
Go ! tell the sloth how o'er the distant plain
Tears the wild horse with high, far-flowing mane.
Go ! tell the stretching desert's sweeping sands,
Of blooming verdure in well-watered lands ;
They'll heed you not—no wished - for change will
          come—
The sparrow still will cling to lowly home,
The bat, still flit along its darkened place,
The sloth, ne'er quicken its slow-dragging pace.

The burning deserts still with parched sands roll,
And so it seems with every human soul :
By nature wicked—miserable its state,
Imbued with envy, malice, wrath, and hate ;
No genial soil a better growth improves,
All things must change ere man his neighbour loves."

" 'Tis true a change must in the heart take place,
Ere perfect Love can show her holy face.
Friends may mislead, mean selfishness may work,
And treachery in dearest bosoms lurk.
But power divine can scatter every ill,
Shine thro' the gloom—with peace the dark soul fill ;
O ! pray and wait, and hail the first faint gleams,
They'll gain in strength, end in heart-warming beams.
Then, what seems now so hard to understand
Plain will appear as ocean, sky, or land ;
And while sin's ravages we all deplore,
We'll love the *man* and hate the *sin* the more.

O holy Love ! thy pale beam's fading ray
Hath not entirely died from earth away—
Essence of heaven ! still from thy pitying eye,
The starting tear falls at the heart-drawn sigh

Thy soft hand lingers on the throbbing head,
Wipes the moist cheek, and tends the sufferer's bed;
Thy sacred finger upward pointing yet,
Bids us to hope, to cease each vain regret;
Existing evil only tends to prove
We've yet to reach thy sparkling halls, O Love!"

THE FIDDLER AND
THE FAYS.

The Fiddler and the Fays.*

A Tale of Mona.

THEY told me of sweet Mona's Isle
    Reclining in the seas,
Where purple hills majestic rise,
    And health dwells in the breeze.

They told me of the foamy waves
    Which dashed against the hill;
They told me of the bright green bays
    Transparent pure and still.

They told me of old castles brave,
    And mentioned many names
Of noble Manxmen, and they told
    'Bout many beauteous dames.

They told me of the King of Man,
    The lordly Derby he
Who erst did hold, and still retained,
    This fair gem of the sea.

---

* This Poem is founded on a story related by Waldron in his
description of the Isle of Man, folio, 1731.

They told me of sweet sylvan plains,
　　Where sportful lambs abound ;
They told me of weird monuments,
　　And shady dells profound.

They told me too of music sweet
　　That quivered thro' each vale ;
Of glorious song floating along
　　On every passing gale.

They made me long to see the Isle
　　Reclining in the seas,
Where purple hills majestic rise,
　　And health dwells in the breeze.

*　　　*　　　*　　　*　　　*

The sea is calm, and lazily
　　The snowy sea-bird twirls ;
The wavelets creep close to my feet,
　　And break in hoary curls.

The drowsy sun his red face hides
　　In ocean's slumb'ring breast,
A gentle breeze came sighing by
　　As lulling him to rest.

And with the breeze a Fisher's boat
   Came sailing near the beach—
Came sailing on so near and close
   It seemed within my reach.

" Where are you for, my fisher boy,
   Where bound so late to-day ? "
" Where bound ? " quoth he, "to Mona's Isle,
   To Douglas' sparkling bay."

" Bring hither then your boat, my boy,
   For I would hie away ;
I long to see fair Mona's Isle,
   And Douglas' sparkling bay."

The Fisher spoke, and then the boat
   Came noiselessly along ;
I sat beside the Fisher's boy
   And listened to his song.

With me I had an old tried friend,
   A violin I loved,
Which had to me in weary hours
   Sweet solace often proved.

Q

The thick'ning gloom soon darker grew,
  But sparkling gems of light,
Like love-lit eyes beamed from above
  And sanctified the night.

And then for sev'ral hours the sea
  Shone like to liquid gold,
And fiery bubbles tipped the waves
  As over them we rolled.

At length an upward show'r of light
  Bathed the awaiting sky,
Closing the myriad eyes of night,
  Glittering far on high.

And away in the dim horizon
  A tiny spec was seen ;
The man outstretch'd his hard brown hand :
  " There's Mona bright and green."

Thro' lucid waters clear we sailed,
  By headlands rough and bold ;
I leaped with joy on the fairy Isle
  Of which I had been told.

I leaped with joy like prisoner
　　From long confinement free ;
Sang a song to the morning breeze,
　　Which whistled merrily.

*　　　*　　　*　　　*　　　*

The yellow corn was ripening,
　　The Autumn dews were near,
And I had stay'd in Mona's Isle
　　One happy blithesome year.

And often had my simple lay
　　Been heard by purling streams,
Which rippled o'er their shiny stones
　　In sweet unconscious dreams.

All that I saw seemed fair and fresh,
　　From Nature's bounteous hand,
The boulders bare—the verdant hills
　　And stretching pasture land.

The balmy air was rich with sweets
　　From flow'ry bank and lea,
And nodding trees joined in the hum
　　Of roving honey bee.

The Manxmen too were tall and strong,
　　A brave and manly race ;
The maidens coy and beautiful,
　　Just suited to the place.

But both the young and old believed
　　That in their sea-girt Isle,
Dwelt troops of Elves, who oftentimes
　　The innocent beguile.

I sometimes laughed—but they looked stern,
　　And earnestly would tell
Of strange sights seen—strange noises heard,
　　On pasture hill and dell.

And oft beneath the trellised porch,
　　With woodbine covered o'er,
Whose fragrance filled the humble cot,
　　Thro' casement and thro' door,

A bowl well filled with water clear,
　　The girls with solemn face,
Would snugly put, and this was called
　　The fairies' bathing place.

I could not think, that what I heard
   Was even partly true,
Until one eve there happenèd
   What I'll relate to you.

     *   *   *   *   *

Blythe Christmas-tide was near at hand,
   That love-inspiring time,
And leafless trees stretched forth their limbs
   All crusted o'er with rime.

Alone I watched the murky clouds,
   Thick gathering over-head,
A figure small came softly near,
   And thus to me he said—

" You play and you sing to the hills,
   You sit beside the brook,
Will you play a tune for me, friend,
   Down by yon heathy nook ?

And I to you will give, my friend,
   This gold within my hand ;
We love to hear your merry strains
   Resounding thro' our land."

He passed to me a well-filled purse,
  With kind persuasive look,
And I resolved with him to go,
  Unto the heathy nook.

I took the gold—his kindly eye,
  Shone on me for awhile,
His face then changed to pallid hue,
  And sickly came his smile.

" Adieu," he said, " we'll meet to-night."
  Dread horror froze my blood,
He sunk into the hard crisp soil,
  Where just before he'd stood.

" Now God in mercy save my soul,"
  Thro' chattering teeth I cried ;
Rather than have his horrid gold,
  I would that I had died.

But there it lay within my hand,
  Enclosed in silken purse,
Around I dare not look for fear
  Of Heav'n's blighting curse.

At last I summoned to my aid
 What reason I had left,—
For this mistake all blessings could
 From me not be bereft.

I wandered timidly away,
 Unto the Parson's place ;
Perchance some comfort he might give,
 And words of soothing grace.

The minister heard solemnly
 All that I had to say,
" A woeful thing," quoth he at last,
 " Has happen'd you to-day.

" Yet as the gold thou hast retained,
 And promise fairly giv'n ;
Go—keep thy word—but nothing play,
 Save psalms and songs of heav'n."

But little comforted I went,
 And as the time drew near
My poor heart failed, my cold flesh crept,
 With dread mysterious fear.

I would have prayed, but other thoughts
  Disturbed my heated brain :
And now close by, in moonlight dim,
  The figure stands again.

He spoke—but I could not reply,
  He beckoned me to follow.
I slunk along, with falt'ring steps,
  To dark and distant hollow.

No house was there, but interlaced
  The ragged bushes grew ;
On every side were fir-clad hills,—
  And squeaking night-bats flew.

A rocky fragment then he found,
  And bade me seated be,
And play—not to the senseless rocks,
  But to his company.

" Where is your company ? " I asked,
  " But you and I are here ; "
" My friends are now all rising fast,
  From coffin, grave, and bier.

They come from grot and cave and tower,
  And cemetery's shade ;
From human ills and grave-yard chills,
  To dance in yonder glade.

They spring from the suicide's wounds,
  Stiff and cold and gory ;
From the murderer's writhing frame,
  Whether young or hoary.

They are forced from the drunkard's teeth,
  By fire that burns within ;
And scraggy misers join our crew,
  With noisy jingling din.

So play some merry airs," he said,
  " Help us to merry be ;
They care for naught, they think of naught,
  Our merry company."

And then a horrid thing crept by,
  Of hideous toad-like mien ;
Leaped to his hand, and both dissolved
  In the glimmering sheen.

*　　*　　*　　*　　*

R

The moonbeams, struggling thro' the gloom,
With sickly pallor fell,
The trembling shadows of the firs
Reached half-way o'er the dell.

Thin vap'ry forms came flitting by,
And plainly could I see,
The gambols of the elfin crew,
Who wished a tune from me.

I struck a soft, low, plaintive note ;
The spectral forms stood still,
And seemed to grasp the quiv'ring sound
Escaping up the hill.

I filled the valley's fern-grown deeps
With sacred songs and airs,
The misty shades fled here and there,
Singly and in pairs.

An unseen owl high midst the trees,
With fitful hootings strong,
Disturbed the place, yet upward still
Floated the sacred song.

The list'ning fays together pressed,
    Each one to other hissed,
They pressed so close that soon they seemed
    A cloud of hov'ring mist.

They seemed a cloud of hov'ring mist,
    Of dim, unearthly gleam,
And glitt'ring from the cloud I saw,
    As in some horrid dream,

Twinkling eyes like fiery jets,
    And faces deathly pale ;
Distinct they were, and yet they were
    One grey unbroken veil.

Cold drops now stood upon my brow,
    All power my frame had lost,
I might have been a murderer
    Before his victim's ghost.

But struggling with myself I said,
    'Why should I think of harm?'
And played again a sacred tune,
    And played again a psalm.

The living cloud then denser grew,
 It came close by my head,
With wind-like moans and chatterings,
 Like voices from the dead.

It nearer came and o'er me hung,
 Chill tremblings seized each limb,
I sat 'neath a load of spirits—
 My senses crushed and dim.

 * * * * *

The cold, bleak wind did colder blow,
 The cloud was not in sight,
I gazed around, but nothing found,
 Save the cold, starry night.

Nothing above but moonlit space,
 Nothing around but air,
Nor dark-brown rocks, nor flitting bats,
 Nor tap'ring pine nor fir.

But far below in slumber lay,
 The peaceful hamlets still,
And far below the valley lay,
 Nestling its silver rill.

With mind o'erwrought, and body bruised,
  I hastened down to tell
What strange things I had heard and seen
  In that dark, mystic dell.

How from the dismal place I reached
  That lone and silent height,
Is the greatest mystery to me,
  Of that unhallowed night—

Is the greatest mystery to me,
  Of that unhallowed night—
And I dare no more laugh, as before,
  At elves in the dim moonlight.

But when the Tempter's power I feel,
  I hum or sing a psalm,
For sacred song brings sacred thought,
  Which shields us from the harm.

HOPE OF THE LAND.

Hope of the Land.

" ' HOPE of the land ! ' what means this fulsome
     phrase,
To England's heart in these enlightened days ?
Gone are the times, when courtiers smooth and bland,
Obsequious hirelings, ruled our down-trod land.
Past are the days when flattery's wiles received
Bounty which should the virtuous have relieved.
Your Monarchs' and your Princes' power hath
     passed—
The Majesty of Labour's owned at last.
Why then, base scribblers, propagate your lies ?
Abjure your nonsense, and, in time, be wise ;
The nation's hope lies in no prince's life—
Princes at best mean but expense and strife ;
The working-man will his own ruler be,
He hath the power to make our country free.
Why should his brawny arm the hammer wield ?
Why should his brow the blackened sweat-drops
     yield,

To foster Royalty—support a crown—
And crush his wife and tender children down?
' Hope of the Land !' O ye insidious knaves—
If he's our hope we must be simple slaves."

" Hold, recreant muse ! is this that mournful strain,
Which thou for days hast whispered through my
          brain ?
Is this that solemn, sympathetic note,
The troubled warblings of thy throbbing throat ?
Is British feeling thus to be expressed ?
Are these the thoughts that animate our breast ?
If so, O ! cease my Muse, no more indite ;
Away my pen, I may no further write."

Methought my Muse with cheerful smile replied,
" I've travelled o'er the country far and wide,
Few towns or hamlets where I have not been,
And lingered spell-bound o'er each mournful scene.
Erin's sweet isle, from north to south, I've roved,
And o'er fair Scotia, by us all beloved.
And far away, across the rolling main,
To where bright India spreads her sunny plain—
Or where Australia, in more distant seas,—
Blooms 'neath the breath of cooler-tempered breeze.

From ev'ry land I've heard the mourning throng
Pray for and bless the burden of my song.
With few exceptions ev'ry fond heart yearns
With sympathy, and to his sick couch turns.
'Tis here alone, beneath his native skies,
That brutish feelings startle and surprise.
But O ! how vain the churlish few who speak,
And babble forth their treason week by week ;
Whose prate of ruling is but mere pretence,
Despised by all, laughed at by common sense.
These feel their rule—the wives they talk about—
Their ragged children, running in and out
Of squalid homes—where chatt'ring hunger shows
Her grinning teeth, and mocks at sweet repose.
These know the men, and knowing, curse the
            hour
In which they first were led to taste the power
Of those who leave them at the work-house gate,
Whilst they in drunken speech abuse the state.
Their rabid nonsense shameful 'tis to see
Gain thro' the press such wide publicity ;
Nor could it ever shock the public view,
Were those in power, as honest, good or true
As they might be—'tis useless here to ask
Whose approbation wears a frowning mask.

We all must know whose covert master-mind
By double-dealing these poor wretches blind,
Whose eloquence his followers betrays—
They, blindly led, pursue his dangerous ways—
Whose dark resentment brooks no honest fear,
Who frames a law, and breaks it in a year;
Whose mighty mind, courageous at all times,
Shrinks from the test of childish pantomimes.
How strangely sensitive that leader's mind,
Who daily hears from baronet and hind,
Treason's bold speech poured forth to gaping crowd,
Which greet the ribald's talk with cheering loud.
Says 'traitors such as these must be exempt
From power of law, and "punished with con-
          tempt,"'
Whilst his, forsooth, and his colleagues' fair fame,
No joking clown or pantaloon must name;
But let them pass—Briton's true sons will yet,
Their country's house in perfect order set.

*   *   *   *   *

Hope of the land, low laid by wasting pain,
O for a hand to bring thy strength again!
O for some charmed Nepentha's subtle power
To change the aspect of each ling'ring hour.

All we possess, and all bright Science knows,
Seems impotent to bring to thee repose.
For still, alas ! the dire disease remains,—
Distils its poison thro' thy fevered veins.
Sweet sleep appears for ever to have fled,
And hungry death seems hov'ring o'er thy head.
O spare him, heaven ! the stricken household cries,
O spare him, heaven ! the trembling land replies ;
Unnumbered hearts bowed low in silent grief,
Pray for their Prince's and their own relief ;
O could a nation's love but aid him now,
Soon would bright health replace the pallor of his
    brow.

I've seen a widowed mother's only son,
Lie gasping, writhing—his pained couch upon ;
I've seen her lips pressed to his burning cheek—
The mighty woe she felt, but could not speak ;
The nightly vigils when with noiseless tread
She moved about—or wept beside his bed.
The silent prayers that left her humid eye,
On pleading glances at the distant sky—
Now, once again, methinks, I see her stand,
A widow's hopes and fears—alternate move the land.

   December 1871.

     *   *   *   *   *

The brooding mists have gone, cheerful and bright,
A smiling morn bursts thro' the ebon night.
A fond relief each weary bosom hails,
And joyous murmurings float upon the gales.
The fight with Death—fought on the very verge
Of his dark confines—fought amidst the surge
Of that dread river, emblem of the grave,
So terrible to timid souls or brave,
Is over now, and life has won! has won!
With joy Britannia hails her Ruler and her Son.—
O dearer now than e'er thou wert before,
One humble lay for thee we would out-pour;
Little we thought ere sickness' hand oppressed
How true to thee was every English breast.
How close inwoven in our being thou
We ne'er did know—we ne'er did feel till now.
Hope of the land—arise, renew thy strength.
Thy worth appears—thy merit's felt at length.
Emblem of order—corner-stone of peace,
Our hope in thee must from this time increase.

*   *   *   *   *

O thou our Queen, our Mother, and our friend,
Our hearts must mourn the troubles thy heart
        rend;

Loved for thyself, thy virtues and thy throne,
When pain is thine—then pain we too must own.
Respectful homage now we gladly pay—
The rule of love, how pleasant to obey—
Whilst humbly bowed to list'ning heaven we raise,
A fervent song of thankfulness and praise.

January 1872.

A VISION OF PEACE AND WAR.

T

A Vision of Peace and War.

THE mellow twilight clasps a busy world,
    Though to the hazy mountain-tops still cling
The glories of a now-departed sun.
Young Edwin stands upon a verdant slope
Of velvet grass, unconscious of the change
From light to twilight, and from this to dark.
And one by one the tiny birds retire ;
And one by one the noiseless angels hang
Their holy beacons in eternal space ;
And one by one the distant noises cease ;
And to the earth the vapoury dew steals
Slowly down, bringing refreshment on its wings.
Still Edwin stands, until a gentle hand
Soft laid upon his arm calls back his thoughts
From wand'ring o'er the far-off golden fields
Of boyish hope, with honour, beauty, love,
And glory strewed ; and thus a plaintive voice :
" Dear Edwin, come ! The night is damp and chill,
And now the bounteous heaven is breathing forth

Its ev'ning blessing. and the silent dew
Bears it to earth.   Come to thy cottage home.
Would that for years that cottage roof might shield
My Edwin's head.   Dear Edwin ! I have had
Seven fine boys, and from my outstretched arms
That spirit of decay, relentless Death,
Hath torn them—and of my once-proud boys
Remains but you ! And now, when from my head
Are hanging but a few, thin silv'ry hairs,
And Care, and Pain, and Toil, and Trouble great
Have done their work, and left my once strong
    frame
In feeble helplessness, with but one prop
On which to lean in this wide, cheerless world,
You leave me, and with careless, cruel hand
Dash from my bending frame its one support,
Leaving my broken heart to die alone.
O Edwin, stay ! for soon my weary head,
Now pillowed on your breast, will pillowed be
On the bosom of the cold earth for aye."
Young Edwin stooped, and kissed the furrowed brow
Pressed to his heart, and wiped the tear away
That trembling stood upon his mother's cheek,
And led her to her quiet cottage home.

*   *   *   *   *

The lucid sunbeams through the heated air
Cleave their swift course, and on the scorched-up
    earth
Descend with parching power and crack the soil.
Young Edwin wanders o'er the crisping grass,
And with a soft and melancholy gaze
Views the deep valleys and the golden hills,
Which he has viewed a thousand times before,
But which he soon must leave for far-off land :
For Edwin had resolved to go abroad—
Sick of a quiet life 'midst rural scenes—
To seek for glory on the battle-field.
He now reclines beneath a tall, broad oak,
Where, shielded from the mid-day's sick'ning heat,
He gently falls asleep.
            And now before
His wakeful mind, as there enchained he lay,
A vision came.   And lo ! two mighty hills
Divided by a valley dark and deep—
The left with sides precipitous and black,
Uncultivated, torn, and ragged rock ;
The right with pastures of the brightest green,
Where cattle grazed and merry children played,
Where people walked and seemed entirely bent
On industry, and love, and pleasure sweet.

And Edwin lay upon a high green mound,
Which rose from out the valley, and which stood
Just half-way 'tween these hills so much unlike:
And from the depths on his right hand arose
Sweet songs of mirth, and happiness and joy;
And from the depths on his left hand arose
A harsh and horrid din of strife and pain.
High, mounted on two rocky pinnacles,
Reared on the summit of the verdant mound
On whose rich side the speckled cattle grazed,
A throne of peerless hue and beauty stood,
And on it sat an angel from whose face
Beams of refulgent light shot through the air,
And her rich garments of a peerless white
Filled the ambient space with rich perfume.
Her golden hair hung round her drooping wings,
Whose snowy feathers reached full half-way down
The verdant slopes and happy-burdened hill.
And on one side a fruitful olive grew,
And on the other grew a leafy palm;
And these met o'er the glist'ning, gem-like throne.
Around the olive and the leafy palm
Flew many a heavenly cherub fair,
Whose tuneful voices, trained in choirs divine,
Joined in a song the snowy angel sang.

On the high summit of the blackish rock
A rough-hewn platform stood, and on it one
From whose dread face the burdenèd thunder-cloud
Drew back, and, bursting, fell its fiery bolt.
Dark was his visage, and around his seat
Fierce, hissing serpents raised their scaly heads
And shot into the air envenomed fangs.
Dreadful, yet beautiful, his swarthy face :
And from his awful brow, in clustering curls,
His raven hair was flung.   His rolling eye
Was like the blazing sun at summer noon,
And o'er his head a red revolving star
Shone with a glare unknown to mortal ken.
He spoke : and from his lips the hissing words
Rung 'gainst the hills and leaped from crag to crag.

"Let loose my Dogs! I hear a sound,
  A rumbling sound falls on my ear,
  A sudden tremor shakes the ground,
  A threatening murmur hovers round—
  And the nations quake with fear.

'Tis the note of Passion and Hate,
  'Tis the growl of a kingly thief ;

Whose slightest nod disturbs a state—
A million souls may meet their fate
In a day ; and all life is brief.

Let loose my Dogs ! the time has come—
Man's fiercest passion conquers now,
With trumpet's blast and rolling drum
A country's manhood leaves its home,
To be murdered and hurled below.

My red, right hand, with an iron grip,
It must seize them whilst yet afar ;
My bolts asunder their ranks must rip,
And your tongues the streaming gore must sip,
For this is glory—Dogs of War !

My glory's gone ! my days are o'er !
And murder is called by my name,—
Gone with knights who in days of yore
For beauty fought, and what was more,
For Honour—Truth—a country's fame !

Now I'm used by accursed knaves,
A treasury's coffers to fill ;
Mammon's worship's the rule—poor slaves—
They tear up the land and the waves
For Gold, and they murder and kill.

The strongest arm ! the noblest heart !
The greatest heroes of the world
Abhor my name, and take no part
In aught I do—away they start
Whene'er my banner is unfurled.

Let loose my Dogs ! their iron jaws
By reptiles now are called in use ;
Who battle not in noble cause,
Tear them ! let vulture's beaks and claws
Finish the sordid, vile refuse ! "

* * * * *

Then from the dark abyss arose a howl,
And Edwin shuddered in his troubled sleep—

" We come ! we come ! from our much-dreaded home !
Our signals of fire we see in yon dome ;
Our demons are ever ready to roam,
                        Lead on !
Lead us to homes where wretched mothers weep,
And sorrow robs the weary eyes of sleep,
And dire distresses nightly vigils keep.
                        Lead on !

                                        L

Lead us to lands where shiv'ring famine roams,
Where hungry mortals dwell in empty homes,
And weep and wait for him who never comes—

Lead on."

*   *   *   *   *

Then Edwin heard a soft sweet strain arise,
And thus the Angel, o'er whose golden hair
The waving olive kissed the leafy palm :—

"Come heav'n-born Cherub !—Lo ! the joyful sound
Of peace and love sighs in the air around,
And precious fruits make glad the ladened ground.

Lead on !

When Sol is sinking—when the twilight grey
With cooling breath blows out the flickering day—
Where happy lovers roam o'er pleasant way—

Lead on !

Lead me to seas upon whose foamy breast
A noble fleet of merchant vessels rest,
Burdened with goods from north, south, east, and west.

Lead on !

To palace great, whose hallowed halls contain
The trophies of Industry's peaceful reign,
Great triumphs of the hand, the heart, the brain—

Lead on !

Lead me where joy and happiness increase—
Where love, contentment, virtue, never cease—
While cherubs sing the happiness of peace ! "
            " Lead on !"

The last strain of the snowy Angel's voice
Had died away, when sleep flew from his eyes,
And Edwin walked upon the crisping grass,
Revolving in his mind what he had seen.
But yesterday he thought that Glory reigned,
And Glory only on the battle-field !
But now he saw that Avarice and Death
Were the chief actors in the wretched scene :
While Peace was crowned with happiness and love.
And Edwin stayed at home, and made the heart
Of his aged mother happy ; for she knew
That Edwin would not leave her, but would live
In peace within their quiet cottage home.

THE FALLEN ONE'S
RETURN.

The Fallen One's Return.

"OH forgive me, mother! for I own my sin!
My poor heart with anguish bursts its bounds
within.

O forgive me, sister, send me not away!
Open to me, brother, I'm as cold as clay!"

She feebly knocked, and listened at the cottage door;
"It is I," she whispered, and knocked again once
more.

" O mother, dearest, open! brother, sister, come!
Your poor deluded Ellie wants to die at home.

Open quickly, mother; Death's billows o'er me roll;
I feel the cold wind blowing on my naked soul."

Softly ope'd the door, but the mother could not speak;
Freely coursed the hot tears adown her withered
cheek.

She clasped the half-starved daughter to her loving
     breast,
And kissed the marble brow, now seemingly at rest.

" Ellie, I have waited, for many, many years ;
Sad at heart and weary—feeding on my tears.

I have wandered up and down in the city's glare,
Looking, Ellie, for you, but I couldn't find you there.

But now you've come, my heart may taste a little joy,
'Tho' in the graveyard rest my other girl and boy.

Kiss your poor old mother, lift up awhile your head."
No response was uttered—she spoke unto the dead.

     *   *   *   *   *

As they pass you, pity them ; oft unwillingly they
     roam,
Whilst they curse the heartless wretch who decoyed
     them from their home.

MY LITTLE ONE.

x

My Little One.

HIS little face lies close to mine.
   His pretty face so soft and fair :
His blue eyes blink—his blue eyes shine,
His little hand plays in my hair.

He lifts his head—his tiny mouth.
With sweet lips pursed and very red.
Soft as air from the dewy south,
Sweet as the violet's crispy bed.

Asks for a kiss with playful eyes—
Those pretty eyes so bright and blue,
Remind me of the summer's skies,
Whilst the kisses speak of morning dew.

He crows ! he sings ! he frets ! he plays !
And loves and clips with chubby arms,
Showing his pretty winning ways—
Laughing at noises and alarms.

So may my cherub always be,
A symbol of confiding love,
And may I trust as he trusts me,
The Father of us all above.

ODE

IN COMMEMORATION OF THE

Shakspere Tercentenary.

April the 23rd, 1864.

Shaksperean Tercentenary Ode.

THE poor, frail body lives but for a day,
    Then dies, and mingles with its parent clay ;
Not so the mind, whose high ennobled powers
Reign far beyond the reach of fleeting hours—
Which, as from vast eternity they roll,
Big with fresh gifts for ev'ry living soul,
Own the supremacy of mental might,
And chant its praises in their mystic flight.
Time seems to linger on a drooping wing,
The praises of the great to sweetly sing ;
And as each hoary century disappears,
Those names remain that to its early years
Lent beaming lustre—living fresh and green,
Untouched by aught—unchanged in changing scene.
Each year adds dust unto the mouldering heap,
Each day adds sleepers to the hosts that sleep ;
But mind immortal heeds not death's cold frown,
And bids the years add laurels to its crown.
So, when men's handiwork rots with decay,
The works of mind new beauties but display,

Forming the thoughts of thousands yet unborn—
Shedding sweet radiance o'er our life's young morn,
And teaching in a multitude of ways
How best our fallen faculties to raise.
Together do sweet truth and knowledge grow,
Around their base wide streams of wisdom flow—
Let all men taste the fruit—drink of the stream—
And purer light within their breast must beam—
Until this mighty world, from pole to pole,
True greatness finds in mind, and heart, and soul.
Then wonder not, ye nations, that our land
Beholds with conscious pride great Shakspere stand
Once more pre-eminent before the face
Of gazing multitudes : each line they trace
Of his impassioned verse, or happy song,
And own that laurel crowns to him belong.

    .   .   .   .

Best loved of bards ! tho' now so long since dead,
Another wreath we clasp around thy head.
The sweetness of thy strains we think we hear—
In fancy see thy well-known face appear—
So full of majesty and earnest thought,
Endorsing ev'rything thy writings taught.
Well may thy country wait to greet the morn
Whereon the Prince of Earth's sweet bards was born ;

And as bright Phœbus wings his upward flight,
Ten thousand voices hail his beaming light,
Whilst music, song, and dance make glad the earth,
Proclaiming loud the day of Shakspere's birth.

How would the muses gather round his bed,
Bedeck his lowly couch and pillowed head;
And gentle zephyrs kiss his baby face,
Who was to prove the lord of bardic race.
His mighty works, and his untarnished fame,
Will live so long as Britain has a name—
Will live not only in the classic groves,
Where knowledge dwells, or studious scholar moves—
Not only in the homes of rich and great,
Where splendid volumes lie in courtly state—
Not only in the scenes on mimic stage,
Tho' there he pictured forth each passing age;
They live enshrined within the hearts of those
Who love the thistle, shamrock, or the rose.
The rustic swain will tune his plaintive song,
To happy milk-maid as they stroll along;
And scarce a cottager in English Isle
But reads his page—and his own life the while.
His fame rests not on keen-eyed critic's pen,
Nor on the breath of great or little men,

Y

Nor on the patronage of rich or proud,
Nor on the wild huzza of boisterous crowd.
It lives wherever Britain's sons are found—
On Afric's plain or Iceland's frozen ground :
It lives upon itself—a noble life,
Above decay—beyond all earthly strife.
His beauteous thought, the songs he sweetly
    sung.
Will ever keep his mem'ry fresh and young ;
His tuneful numbers rolled from cultured mind,
And fell like heav'n's soft whispers to his kind,
Replete with beauty, purity, and grace,
Immortal gifts unto our mortal race.
No subject was for his great mind too high,
His soaring genius mounts the farthest sky,
Fearlessly views a dread eternity,
And speaks of things that were and are to be—
Places before our now enraptured sight
Fair visions of true love and pure delight ;
Now bids our eyes let fall the scalding tear
On worth, down-trampled to a gory bier ;
Now horrifies our sense with murd'rous scene,
Now gently leads us over pastures green.
The howling elements obey his will,
Bending, subdued, unto his magic skill ;

Faith: its Pleasures, Trials and Victories,

AND OTHER POEMS.

BY

JAMES WARLOW.

Pp. 194, *with Portrait of Author. Square Crown 8vo., price* 21s., *cloth extra, with gilt edges.*

" *Faith, and other Poems,* is the title of a magnificently bound work by Mr. JAMES WARLOW. Publishers—*Longmans, Green & Co., London.* The author of this work is highly gifted with poetical genius of no common order, and to follow him in his flights of fancy amidst charming scenes, described in exquisitely beautiful language, is no ordinary treat. For the libraries of the *élite* who delight to revel in the regions of poetic raptures, ' Faith, and other Poems' is well worthy of a place of honour."—

Protestant Standard.

Extract from a letter written by the Rev. J. F. STEVENSON, D.D., LL.B., Brixton, London, and kindly placed at the Author's disposal :—

"I have read much of the fine poem entitled ' Faith,' and also some of the shorter poems in the beautiful volume. They seem to me to be full of a truly poetic insight and fire, and I cannot doubt that the Author has a noble literary career before him."

A few copies of this Edition may still be obtained.

A limited number of copies of the above Work, beautifully bound and printed on extra thick toned paper, are now offered at 5s. per volume.

Dread demons forth from loathsome dens appear,
Foul reptiles docile crawl and hover near ;
Hypocrisy her hateful sin foregoes,
And slander's many tongues the truth disclose.
His pen presents to us things as they are—
The good and pure—bright as the silv'ry star,
While guilt and wickedness his page displays
In all the filthy meanness of their ways.
His native genius, polished by his art,
Stands all alone without one counterpart,
And brings like ocean's waves from ev'ry land
Great priceless treasures to our outstretched hand.
He knew the workings of our passions deep,
Could lull them softly to a gentle sleep ;
Could make them rise with billows fierce and
    strong,
Enslaving us to whom they should belong.
Scarce one small thought passed thro' the human
    breast,
Nor wish, nor fond desire, tho' unexpressed,
That doth not in his lucid works appear,
As 'twere ourselves had placed experience there.
Scarcely a flower that bloomed in British air,
Scarcely a worm that crawled her damp ground
    bare,

Scarcely a phase of human life below,
But to his mind some hidden truth did show;
He gathered lessons from all things he saw,—
Found all things formed for good by Nature's law;
With eye of Poet saw the hand Divine
In things both small and great supremely shine.

Tho' Shakspere fought not on the gory field,
Tho' he ne'er carried helmet, sword or shield,
Yet 'midst our heroes must he take his place,
Standing with mighty champions face to face.
His noble banner, when 'twas once unfurled,
Proved him for e'er the chief in lettered world;
He wrote, and rendered victory secure
For ever in the field of literature.
His name will live with those of leaders brave,
Who fought on bloody field or mighty wave,
Who find the actions of their dreaded swords
Proclaimed by Fame in loud soul-stirring words.

But now three centuries away are flown
Since first his voice on earth's great stage was known—
Since first his tiny body helpless lay—
Since first his infant spirit saw the day;

Yet he seems living, nor can ever die
Whilst earth loves truth or sweetest minstrelsy.
But though our mind with admiration scan
The well-loved writings of this glorious man,—
See the great knowledge his large soul possessed,
And note how beauteously his thoughts are dressed ;
View his deep insight into others' thought,
As if by aid Divine he had been taught
All Nature's secret workings to explore,
And ken her deep designs minutely o'er.
See his imagination's onward flight
Thro' scenes of darkness or transcendent light,
Thro' scenes of infamy, and sin, and woe,
Where pity weeps for life so mean and low ;
Thro' scenes of love, and purity, and peace,
Where happiness and bliss seem ne'er to cease ;
Thro' scenes of horrid murder, where the blade
Of dire assassin works in darkened shade ;
Thro' scenes of revelry and foolish rage,
Thro' scenes where folly laughs at wisdom sage,
Thro' scenes where true philosophy is found,
Thro' scenes where mercy sits enthroned and
    crowned,
Thro' scenes where fancy holds ungoverned sway,
And beaming fairies sparkle in array,—

We will remember all to him was given
By the Upholder of the earth and heaven.
So while our Shakspere's memory we sing,
We'll worship Him who formed the Poet's King.

ELLEN'S PRESENT.

Ellen's Present.

An Idyl.

'TWAS Christmas Eve, and from the cheerless sky
    Fell heavily large flakes of virgin snow ;
And all the trees were hung with spotless white—
Ev'ry lane was quiet, and stillness slept
On each receding vale and mist-crowned hill.
All was so quiet that quick fancy heard
The flakes descend and crisp upon their bed.
And happy Ellen—happy because good—
Peered thro' the crimson curtains at the night,
And saw the snow-flakes falling thick and fast.
And Ellen thought about the happy homes
Where Yule logs blazed, and threw their ruddy light
Upon the cheerful faces all around.
And Ellen pictured to herself the sire,
With white locks scattered over rustic brow,
Gazing with honest pride upon the boys
Good Father Christmas had restored to him.
And Ellen thought she heard the merry laugh
As each one gave his Christmas toast or song,

Z

And Ellen's fancy saw the good old dame,—
With grandchild nestling snugly in her lap,—
Attentive to the noise of youth and maid,
And thinking her young days had come again.
And Ellen's heart felt happy when she thought
Of others' happiness and peaceful mirth.
And happy Ellen—happy because good—
Still stood and gazed upon the falling snow.
But now she thought about the dreary homes
Where poverty and want and sickness dwelt;
And Ellen pictured the damp floor and walls,
The broken windows and the fireless grate.
And Ellen thought she saw the drifting snow
Beat thro' the broken panes and 'neath the door,
And melt upon the couch where suffering lay.
And Ellen felt unhappy when she thought
Of others' misery and others' want.
Now Ellen had that happy Christmas Eve
Sent presents round the village where she lived
To all the villagers, however poor;
But Ellen had forgotten to send forth
A present to a poor infirm old dame,
Who lived some little way from Ellen's house.
And as she gazed upon the falling snow
She thought about this woman—lame and poor.

And Ellen got some wine and fruit and cake,
And put them in a basket, and went forth,
Enveloped in a cloak whose ample folds
Kept off the snow that still came quickly down.
And Ellen reached the cot, and gently raised
The unresisting latch, and looked within.
And Ellen thought she heard a sob and moan
Come from some inner chamber, and she went
To where the troubled sound proceeded from.
The poor old dame lay helpless on a bed,
And by her side a pale thin maiden sat,
Who threw her arms around the old dame's neck,
And sobbed, and leaned her head upon the bed.
Ellen approached, and raised the weeping girl,
And asked the meaning of the scene she saw.
The sobbing maiden told her simple tale—
Of how her mother had—from want and cold—
Been sick ; and how they both had waited long
To get their Christmas present from the Hall—
But it came not, and she was weeping then
Because her mother, sick from cold and want,
Could not procure her wonted Christmas treat.
Kind Ellen's heart reproached her when she heard
The sobbing maid, and saw the sick old dame.
She took some wine, and with her gentle hand

Gave each to drink ; and Ellen took the fruit
And cake and put them by the old dame's side—
And the poor old dame, and the thin pale maid,
Thanked Ellen deeply with their sunken eyes.
And happy Ellen—happy because good—
Kissed the thin maid, and blessed the poor old dame,
And hurried thro' the quickly falling snow,
Leaving Happiness and sweet Peace behind.

THE MUSE AND THE
ZEPHYRS.

The Muse and the Zephyrs.

" AWAY, gentle Zephyr! loving and kind,
    Hence to bright Flora's home, there you
        will find
Your sportive companions singing in glee.
Away, gentle Zephyr! bring them to me.

On their wings reclining I'll journey above,
I'll sing of beauty, and virtue, and love.
The fair world around us, the scene shall be.
Away, gentle Zephyr! bring them to me.

O! there's many a lyre as yet unstrung,
And there's many a song as yet unsung.
Away—away! the dim future I see,
And bring thy companions closer to me.

There's many a heart still weary and torn,
There's many a spirit broken and worn.
Away—away! let us all useful be,
And bring thy companions nigh unto me.

We'll join in a song of beauty and love,
They'll hear us below tho' we sing it above.
Fly to thy home—near the calm western sea—
And bring thy companions hither to me."

Zephyr.

" I go—yes, I go,
    Sweet Goddess of Song ;
Lightly my airy wings
    Speed me along.
No wild thyme shall tempt me,
    No roses betray—
To do all thy bidding,
    Away—I'm away ! "

Hark to the airy wings,
    Zephyr hath flown—
List to the murmurings
    O'er the hill blown.

Hither he comes again
With a bright spirit train,
 Lightsome and gay,—
Comes ere sweet Echo sings
 'Way—I'm away !

Muse.

" Where have your wand'rings been, Zephyrs so
  bright,
Since last you bore me thro' wavelets of light ?
Come you from lake, or from mountain, or lea,—
What subjects for song have you brought to
  me ? "

1st Zephyr.

" As I passed along,
 O Goddess of Song,
By the sylvan edge of a shaded mere,
 I saw a young child
 Pluck a primrose wild,
The first that had bloomed in the grass this year.
 O they looked so bright
 In the amber light,
By the sylvan edge of the shaded mere."

Muse.

" Alas ! alas ! but the flower is dead,
Crumpled and soiled—'tis hanging its head.
Alas ! alas ! the dim future I see,
The flower and the child seem the same to me."

2nd Zephyr.

" The day 'twas bright and sultry the weather—
I passed o'er a hill-side, blooming with heather;
When suddenly out of the gloomy north,
The spirit of Boreas tumbled forth—
And suddenly too the sky grew dark—
A peal of thunder rang thro' the hills—
A flaming tongue lit by meteor spark
Scorched the heather and lapt up the rills ;—
Glared thro' a gloomy forest of Pines
Where I seldom wander and the sun never shines !

I saw by the light of the lurid tongue,
A figure standing those dark Pines among ;
Thin was his face, and wrinkled, and sear,
Bony the hands spread out in the glare—
There has he dwelt full many a year,
Employing the time in continual Prayer ;
Away from his fellows, for Prayer and Praise—
Is he not an example in these latter days ?"

Muse.

"The Eagle's place is the eyrie high,
The topmost crag and the boundless sky :
In tangled brushwood or secret glen
The cunning Fox may select his den,
But why should Man from his fellows stray,—
In solitude pass his years away ?
There's plenty of work for all to do,
From sin and crime there're plenty to woo ;
And selfish the mind, and mean the man,
Who doth not for all do what he can.
Useless and sad a hermit must be,
And the future shows none of his virtues to me."

3rd Zephyr.

"Away from the valley
I thoughtfully wandered o'erladen with sweets.
Upwards and downwards,
Till I flew townwards,
Where many an alley
Breathes poison and death on the numerous streets.
I wished, as I sped along,
That I had the power of song,

The stern-visaged traders to melt and to cheer;
For ev'rything round was so wretched and drear.
 When lo ! in the city's mist,
 A bright-featured boy I kissed—
Humming the same wish in numbers so true,
 I lingered to listen—
 I saw his eye glisten—
With raptures I oft have noticed in you."

    Muse.

"'Then spread out your filmy wings,
 Cease all your sweet murmurings—
 Let us away to the city's cold mist.
 We'll sing to the busy throng
 Some cheering or useful song,
By the voice of the boy whom our Zephyr hath kissed."

BALLANTYNE, HANSON AND CO.
EDINBURGH AND LONDON.

www.ingramcontent.com/pod-product-compliance
Lightning Source LLC
Chambersburg PA
CBHW030552040726
47497CB00008B/2687